Stories by

ALL THE WAY TO DEATH

This book is edited and designed by the Editorial Committee of *Cultural China* series

Text by Na Duo
Translation by Jiang Yajun
Cover Image by Quanjing
Interior Design by Xue Wenqing
Cover Design by Wang Wei

Editors: Cao Yue, Susan Luu Xiang
Editorial Director: Zhang Yicong

Senior Consultants: Sun Yong, Wu Ying, Yang Xinci
Managing Director and Publisher: Wang Youbu

ISBN: 978-1-60220-259-7

Address any comments about *All the Way to Death* to:

Better Link Press
99 Park Ave
New York, NY 10016
USA

or

Shanghai Press and Publishing Development Company, Ltd.
F 7 Donghu Road, Shanghai, China (200031)
Email: comments_betterlinkpress@hotmail.com

Printed in China by Shenzhen Donnelley Printing Co., Ltd.
1 3 5 7 9 10 8 6 4 2

ALL THE WAY TO DEATH

By Na Duo

Translated by Jiang Yajun

Better Link Press

Foreword

This collection of books for English readers consists of short stories and novellas published by writers based in Shanghai. Apart from a few who are immigrants to Shanghai, most of them were born in the city, from the latter part of the 1940s to the 1980s. Some of them had their works published in the late 1970s and the early 1980s; some gained recognition only in the 21st century. The older among them were the focus of the "To the Mountains and Villages" campaign in their youth, and as a result, lived and worked in the villages. The difficult paths of their lives had given them unique experiences and perspectives prior to their eventual return to Shanghai. They took up creative writing for different reasons but all share a creative urge and a love for writing. By profession, some of them are college professors, some literary editors, some directors of literary institutions, some freelance writers and some professional writers. From the individual styles of the authors and the art of their writings, readers can easily detect traces of the authors' own experiences in life, their interests, as well as their aesthetic values. Most of the works in this collection are still written in the realistic style that represents, in a painstakingly fashioned fictional world, the changes of the times in urban and rural life. Having grown up in a more open era, the younger writers have been spared the hardships experienced by their predecessors, and therefore seek greater freedom in their writing. Whatever category of writers they belong to, all of them have gained their rightful places in Chinese literary circles over the last forty years. Shanghai writers tend to favor urban narratives more than other genres of writing. Most of the works in this collection can be characterized as urban literature with Shanghai characteristics, but there are also exceptions.

Called the "Paris of the East," Shanghai was already an international metropolis in the 1920s and 30s. Being the center of China's economy, culture and literature at the time, it housed a majority of writers of importance in the history of modern Chinese literature. The list includes Lu Xun, Guo Moruo, Mao Dun and Ba Jin, who had all written and published prolifically in Shanghai. Now, with Shanghai re-emerging as a globalized metropolis, the Shanghai writers who have appeared on the literary scene in the last forty years all face new challenges and literary quests of the times. I am confident that some of the older writers will produce new masterpieces. As for the fledging new generation of writers, we naturally expect them to go far in their long writing careers ahead of them. In due course, we will also introduce those writers who did not make it into this collection.

Wang Jiren
Series Editor

Contents

Prelude

This is my last novel, and I'm trying to make it a different one.

I have some pictures from the murder, which will help me write a long enough book. I'm exhausted, fatigued, and dying.

There is nothing special about these pictures. Like many others of their kind, they are a mix of beauty and ugliness. You have to know that the most ruthless is always a companion of the brightest. You're being hypocritical if you only see the bright side.

I travel between the light and the dark, and I know my way around crime. Since you are courageous enough to read my story, I'll be kind enough to peel the layers of skin for you to see the soft and bloody insides.

Shall I start from the back of your left hand?

Will it hurt you? As I write these words, I let out a cynical laugh, and the corners of my mouth are turning up. This is why I'm attractive to you.

I'm the best writer of murder mystery in China—I write about cold-blooded killings. Few readers know how a mystery is different from a thriller. I can tell you a mystery is more than a crime novel in that it goes beyond killing. In my novels it is what comes up when a mixture of the features the northwestern places of Jiayuguan, Dunhuang, Shanshan, Korla, Hetian, and Kashgar is left to ferment adequately. I'm familiar with the northwestern local cultures, or I pretend I am.

But I do hope my fans, who have been reading every story of mine all these years, including you, could see what is deep inside the settings of my work: killing and only killing.

Killings of all types. Involuntary or voluntary ones, brutal or cold-blooded ones, killing of one's own father or son, killing of one's own brother or sister, killing of one's lover.

To understand how a person dies—and why—is the utmost secret.

I'll never talk about this again.

Chapter I Before the Journey

For a second time, I was about to travel along the Silk Road. To be exact, it was the greater part of the routes in China: the four thousand kilometers of it from Jiayuguan Pass in Gansu Province to Kashgar in Xinjiang.

The journey was part of a sales campaign for an energy drink. I got involved simply due to the producer of its advertising agency, a regular reader of my stories. The result of the journey would be an advertising video several minutes long, which would appear online when my next book would be promoted. A win-win for both sides, isn't it? And what I had to do was to mention the journey in my book. I reminded the woman that I was a writer of crime and that killers needed energy drinks to be in their best psychopathic form. She was not convinced, and I had to agree. It would be foolish to refuse the handsome sum of money, as long as I would have absolute control over that world. So we had never lacked people who had a remarkable insight into the nature of the world: evil is the most powerful. It is fresh bait.

"Sir, it would be nice if you could talk about the local cultures of northwestern China on the way." The voice over the phone was soft and sexy, and I began to visualize how her lips and throat moved when she talked.

"But I'm better at telling horrifying stories," I told her,

touching my own throat, smiling.

Then the deal went ahead.

It was what had happened two days before I left. I hung up the phone and switched on my computer. My anti-virus program started its scheduled weekly scan. It was a long and painful process for a machine as old as mine, which I bought nearly ten years before when I started my writing career. It took the once most up-to-date electronic device as long as two minutes to power up. Old and gloomy as it was, the machine had in its black box numerous details of killings, which would curl upwards noisily from the metal cracks when I sat up before it. I hoped I could use it for some more time, at least for another five years.

It turned out it had been infected with a virus, a virulent virus. I was asked if I wanted to delete the file once for all.

I was about to hit "Yes" without thinking anything of it, but I stopped.

I had never seen the file.

Of the thousands of files in the computer, I recognized few of them. I didn't need to know which was which, so long as they worked for me. But the file was under a hidden folder named "Memories." Obviously, it couldn't be an automatically generated folder, and I didn't think I had ever created such a hidden private folder.

There must be some problem.

I copied the "Memories" to a flash disk which I had never used for years and changed it to read-only. Then I ran the anti-virus program again and had the folder safely removed.

I opened the "Memories" in the flash disk.

There were five files and the one with the problem was named "Time," which I opened.

"Time: 1994–1999. Memories to be blotted out. I've locked them up, but I have the key. Never go for them. Never go for them. Never go for them."

It was all in the file.

But an icing chill slid up my spine.

This was apparently written my own way.

1994–1999?

Anyone who knew even very little about me knew that I had lost my memory during those five years. This gave me an air of mystery in the eyes of my readers, and what I may have done in the period had become a topic of their conversations.

It makes an incredible story that a sophomore in high school left home in the summer and never returned until he woke up under a locust tree by the Yulong River. Later he worked as a courier, a doorman, and a book distributor, before his book *Old Well, Eyeballs, and Teeth*, a novel set in the Northwest, went all the way to number one in the 2003 bestseller list in China. In the following years he produced a new book every year, and in 2008 his *Roaming around to Die* caused a sensation in Japan, which helped him become an influential writer in China. It was sarcastic, but natural enough.

Allow me to tell you how others were speculating about what had happened to the teenager. A boy who still had a long way to go before his middle-age, he had been regarded as a hugely successful writer. With a gaunt and gray face and white gloves on, he looked as if he were a forensic expert who was always ready to process a dead body. Reserved at a time but bold at another, he was rather weird and unpredictable. Some critics said that he was a showman, who had made up all his stories, including his loss of memory, only to make a mystery of himself. Others said that he must be a killer to produce stories which were as horrible to read as his, because he claimed from time to time that only a killer knew what a killer was. But the majority of readers believed that his loss of memory must have been essential to his success in mystery stories—he may have had most grotesquely adventurous experience in the five years and every story of his was written when what had happened to him was gradually unlocked in his subconscious. People disagreed, but they all had to admit that he had been a legend.

But I was only who I was.

1994–1999? Yes, it was that five years!

My eyes drifted over to the date when the file was last revised: August 9, 2002.

It was the first of the files listed in time order, and the second one had the name "In Jiayuguan," lasted edited the next day.

I hit it, but a password was required.

Staring at the screen for a moment, I entered the digits from 1 to 8. Wrong password. I punched in 19761225, my birthday, but failed again. Reducing it to a six-digit number—761225—I succeeded.

It was not long, about three to five thousand words, the length of a short story. I finished it in one go before I rose for a cigarette. Coming back to the computer, I hit the third file, "In Dunhuang." A password was needed, I entered the previous one, but it was wrong.

I used a familiar code—my mailbox password, but it didn't work.

I smiled self-deprecatingly before I decided to give it up.

"In Jiayuguan" was a horror story. It was somewhat abstract, but it was horrifying and tragic enough to make compulsive reading. It seemed to be my style.

Yes, it was possibly my own story, but I was a much better writer now. It was written in a similar style as that of my *Old Well, Eyeballs, and Teeth*.

I didn't remember I had written it, but I must admit that I could not tell the stylistic difference between this great story and other ones. That mysterious, anonymous writer must be a genius. I clapped my hands for him or her.

It was interesting that I was writing *Old Well, Eyeballs, and Teeth*, the novel which helped to establish my reputation, in the August of the same year.

It must be more than a coincidence. I didn't believe in coincidence.

I was about to leave in two days. Before my trip to Jiayuguan, our first destination, I needed to figure out the damned file which

I had no idea when entered my computer.

But I needed to take my time. My stories featured a mixture of relaxation and intensiveness, you know.

So was a murder.

I slept like a log at night. After I got up at six in the morning, I cooked myself a breakfast of fried egg, sausage, and a cup of hazelnut coffee with milk. Then I started to write down all potential passwords on a piece of paper.

There were altogether 39 of them. I turned on my computer and began to enter them one by one.

Chapter II In Jiayuguan

The sun sank below the horizon. Like the star, I was plunging into the cold darkness, where a huge net was ready in the chaotic state to catch me.

The encrypted stories in my computer were not the net, but bait.

I had bitten the bait along with the hook.

I felt … that I was part of my own story.

In my stories, heroes had to throw themselves into a trap to be successful. They had to do it in a desperate manner, so that they could choose when to do it.

If they are not struggling for the initiative, they are only playing supporting roles.

For they would be killed in the end.

"You're a beauty, second only to that," I told the woman beside me, pointing to the setting sun.

My silver glove reflected the last ray of the sun.

"Sir, you always have your gloves on, don't you," a man's voice said.

We were approaching Jiayuguan. Zhong Yi, the producer who invited me for the trip, walked beside me. A step ahead of us was a woman of late middle age, with whom I plan to discuss questions of face lifts and Botox injections the next morning at breakfast. Actually, I would suggest to her not to wear any make-up, because she would have more wrinkles by exposing herself for a month in the full sun in the windy desert land, which would only add to her sexiness.

Why?

For the total surface area would increase, which would require a longer time to caress every inch of her cheeks.

Every time I designed a dialog, I would look forward to a repetition of it in the real world.

Oh, I'm sorry I forgot to tell you her name was Chen Aiqin. Or Chen Ailing? She was the representative from the soft drink company, and she was with us to make sure the money was put into good use. Thinking about what would happen to me after our conversation, I lost all my interest.

The guy with glasses was talking to the lady, but he turned his head to us from time to time. He was responsible for taking pictures and shooting videos, but he looked like an amateur. He was Zhong Yi's colleague, and I could see he was an admirer of hers from the way how his eyes followed her. It was understandable, because Zhong Yi was a sexy woman with considerable charm. The videographer was Fan Sicong. Yes, he was the guy who had cut in when I spoke to Zhong Yi. I flashed him a mocking smile.

The one left behind was our driver, Yuan Ye, a name that had once been as popular as Chen Zhaodi, Zhang Aiguo, and Wang Jianguo. Freshly discharged from an army in Xinjiang Province, he was hired for the journey to give them a sense of security.

I didn't have to look, but I knew Zhong Yi's face was creasing into a radiant smile, which I found perfectly charming.

"That is prettier, too." She extended a delicate, long-finger from my right side, pointing in the direction of the city of Jiayuguan.

We headed towards the city, leaving the reddish Gobi Desert behind. A downward passage led to the pass, and what was before us in distance was nothing but the red and yellow three-storied arch over the city gate. As we got closer, we saw the top of the earthen pass wall and then more of it. When we were on the top of the slope, the whole city with its gate was seen.

The city and its surrounding area blended. In the wild were small groups of horses and camels, which stood leisurely or wandered freely, while a train ran slowly in the distance. Many years ago, merchants had travelled through the pass on the Silk Road for wealth, and some of them had never returned, while many riding marauders with bows and arrows lost their lives. My imagination ran wild as I breathed in the air of the ancient battlefield.

Zhong Yi and I walked down the slope toward the pass.

"What did you point at?" I asked her. "It was only a tomb."

"Really, a tomb?" Fan Sicong turned to look at me, arching a brow. It seemed he was a man who was always ready to interject.

"We're going down through a passage, and in no time we'll be in a pit. Don't you think it looks like a tomb? This place is home for hundreds and hundreds of ghosts. Badly wounded people were left here to die, and they struggled for life in vain before their death. So this was a tomb of all tombs in the world."

"Stop!" Zhong Yi cried out.

I smiled. "So don't make any comparison between yourself and the tomb; you're scores of years younger."

"But you made a comparison between the sun and me."

"You did," Fan Sicong cut in. "She's billions of years younger."

"The f--king sun. You see what I mean?" I walked slowly forward, my hands buried in my pockets.

My obviously dirty metaphor left them silent. How interesting.

When we were at the bottom of the passage, all my companions looked up at the huge monster with immense weight. Actually, its weight was meaningless to us, because it has rooted there for such a long time that it became part of the earth.

"This is such a low-lying place, as if the pass town was in a huge crater." It was Zhong Yi who broke the silence.

"For defensive purpose I guess," Fan Sicong said.

I began to laugh out loud.

What I did irritated Fan Sicong, but he suppressed his anger because of my popularity as a writer.

I turned to Yuan Ye and helped him onto the place where we were. "Why don't you tell us what you think?"

"I have no idea," Yuan Ye said with a shy smile. "But I don't think it was for defense. For that purpose it would have been a higher place, which would consume more of the attackers' strength and increase their casualties."

"You must know it," Zhong Yi said, attempting to help Fan Sicong up. "Don't keep us guessing."

"Deposition. When the land got lower, wind from the desert would remove the sand around the town slowly and it became even lower. It has become what it is after so many years."

It would get dark at eight o'clock in Jiayuguan at this time of year. It was about half past seven, and the whole sky would grow dark quickly half an hour later. The town was almost free of tourists.

"Jiayuguan has three parts: the inner town, the outer town, and the protection town, which was a construction with its two ends connected to the town wall before the town gate. The whole place goes from east to west, but the gates between the walls were not on a straight line, but on two lines perpendicular to each other for defensive purpose," I explained.

"Well, you're now a tour guide." Zhong Yi clapped her hands.

I smiled at her before I explained what each gate was for and showed them the horse way leading to the top of the town wall. I asked Fan Sicong whether the horse way was for horses, to make fun of him.

I didn't lead them onto the top of the wall, but walked along it honestly.

We passed the Huiji Gate and walked on to Yanwuchang,

where people gathered in the daytime to watch street performances like shooting and mouse tricks or visited stores where strange rocks were sold. But when we were there the street was almost empty of people. A street magician smiled at us as he repeatedly switched two bowls over a coin. When he swallowed down a metal ball as large as a child's fist and his face was tilted towards the sky, ready to force it out of his mouth, Chen Ailing's eyes rounded in amazement and others appeared even more surprised.

I moved forward alone.

The first story with a password was entitled "In Jiayuguan."

It was a very short piece, but it contained explicit scenes of violence.

We were at the very place, Jiayuguan.

I was approaching the net.

Stepping out of the Guanghua Gate, we were outside the inner town and before us were Guandi Temple, the stage and Wenchang Temple, with the first one stood directly in front the other two.

I walked up to the stage.

Zhong Yi caught up quickly from behind. "You're walking too fast."

I ignored her.

"Is this the stage?" she asked.

"Obviously."

"Why don't you tell us what's special about it?"

"Do you know how to get onto it?"

Built with stone blocks, it was as high as an adult, with a long wooden balustrade. Zhong Yi walked along it to the other side, probably thinking she could see a stair case. But I had been here before and I knew she would be disappointed.

The antithetical couplet in the front of it said "On the stage were vicissitudes of life" and "Among the audience the faithful and unfaithful were identified," with "A virtuous nation" high above between them. On the ceiling was a colored painting with five vertical patterns and twenty-five squares. I had been there, but it was the first time that I realized what in the center of the grid was a t'ai chi, which was encircled by a *bagua*, the Eight Diagrams. The outer ring was divided into sixteen squares, in which were traditional paintings of peonies, bats and the like.

Stepping seven or eight steps back to be ready for a running jump at the stage, I climbed onto it with the help of my feet on the base and my hands holding the wood.

Zhong Yi returned from the other side of the stage when she saw what I was doing. "Oh, so that's how you do it," she said, taken aback.

"It was much easier for those actors and actresses."

The eight doors, with a painting of each of the Eight Immortals on it, were tightly closed. Inside was the backstage, which would not be very large, about one third of the stage in size. I glanced at the doors and turned to smile at Zhong Yi before I pointed to one side of the stage.

"Do you see the hooks? It was where the ladder was placed."

"Are you sure?" She looked up at me.

Bending to a squat and dusting off my gloves, I reached out for her. She hesitated before she put her hand on mine to get onto the stage.

"This was built in the Ming Dynasty. Operas were performed right here, and soldiers sat below the stage. Those officials would be sitting on the opposite building called Wenchang."

"What was the opera?"

"Qin opera."

She looked around. "It's nice to stand here, but are we allowed to do so on a stage from the past?"

I laughed and said we could come down if she felt bored.

She walked toward the edge of the stage before she shook her head, saying it would be even harder to get off it. She turned to look at me, but I was where I had been.

"You know it was raining like this that night."

The sun was no longer seen, and it started to rain.

"This stage has been deserted, standing alone in the grave-like ancient castle. It was completely dark, but we caught a flash of white now and then. It was lightning, silent lightning, without a sound. It didn't help, and you only could feel the pitch darkness all the more, and the many shadows in it as well. A crash of thunder could be heard after a long delay. As the thunder and lightning went on, you could see things you had never seen in the day. It was as if the shadows were woken up and they began to move around in make-up and in full costume. Among the large audience were all soldiers."

"Sir, are you divulging facts or is this part of your new work?" Zhong Yi was moving toward me.

"That night, there were people standing right here. Two people, two men, who were friends, as close as brothers. One of them was where you are."

I spoke rather slowly, as if I was trying to remember what had happened. It was getting even darker, but I still could see the goose bumps on her neck.

"It was so dark that it was hard for them to see each other's face clearly, even though they were close. One of them ..." I pointed to myself and switched to the first and second persons. "I took out an oil lamp and lighted it. 'Why don't we sing a passage?' I suggested. 'Which one?' you asked. 'Let me think about it,' I said before I placed the lamp on your head."

It was actually my hand that was on Zhong Yi's head. She didn't move.

"This is called a head lamp in the art. It is for clowns who have done something wrong. You were consumed with guilt, so you didn't say a word, standing with the lamp on your head. Then I began to paint your face with colors. It was about midnight. Outside, it was raining hard and the wind was moaning. There wasn't a single soul around us in the vast place. The lamp flickered, as if it was floating in the air, but it never went out."

I used my hand, as if it were a brush, to paint her face. But I didn't touch her skin, of course.

"Whose face is it?" she asked when I was painting on her lips.

"Zhang Fei in a local opera. But, you didn't ask that night, allowing me to do whatever I wanted. Of course, you could feel what I was painting. And then I started to sing."

As the opera was loud and passionate, my singing immediately attracted those who had lagged behind and they rushed over to be my audience. Fan Sicong pointed his camera at me and kept pressing the button.

I stopped before long and said, "With the lamp on your head, you didn't move and speak. You knew well what I was singing. It was from a historical opera named *Liu Bei at the Worship Ceremony*, in which Liu as the head of a state was paying his respect to his military commanders Guan Yu and Zhang Fei. With a painted face of Zhang Fei, you were a dead man and needed only to listen to me. I continued to sing until I finished the line 'Why did you kill for it?' or 'Why did you leave us so early?'"

I shrugged as if I had been part the story in the opera, not knowing where to stop.

"I stopped abruptly. While the sound of the wind and shower continued, it seemed a sudden, deadly silence fell over the stage. Not knowing what had happened to me, you turned your head. As the lamp was on your head, you had to do it slowly so that it was there. You turned so slowly that you even could hear the cracking sound from the bones inside her neck. When you finally faced me, I had already a rosin bag in my mouth. I blew on the lamp, and a sheet of flame shot into the air with a loud noise."

"You could only see the fire and the light, nothing else. You had to keep your eyes shut tight."

I flung out my coat towards her face. Leaning her head back, she closed her eyes on impulse. Then I cut her neck gently with my gloved hand, as if it were a knife. While my pinkie slipped over her neck, I could feel through the thin fabric the adrenaline coursing through her veins.

"I slashed your throat, and the blood splattered beyond the stage."

Zhong Yi reacted with hysterical screams. I stepped back

from her, grinning with pleasure.

"Is it fun to frighten a young woman like this?" Fan Sicong interfered. "Are you okay, Zhong Yi?"

Leaving his camera aside, he managed to get onto the stage with the help of the balustrade. After a few unsuccessful attempts, he decided to give up. Feeling like a mess, he looked less aggressive.

Zhong Yi was no longer excited, and she opened her eyes in embarrassment. She clamped her hand against her mouth and then laughed at herself. "Sir, you're an excellent storyteller. I lost myself in it, and it seemed it was something happening right here."

"You're a great listener," I paid her a compliment, before I turned to Fan Sicong. "If you want to get onto this stage, all you have to do is to step back for a run-up. The way you did it doesn't work."

My ironic tone left him looking rather distraught, because he had already given up.

"You know, to do so you have to use the muscles on your waist. You're a young man, but your waist is not strong enough. Do you need my help?" I continued to make fun of him, only to find he was moving back, which actually pleased me.

"It's getting dark, sir. Shall we quickly see what we have here and then go back?" Chen Ailing was trying to ease the situation.

"Why don't you come down, with the help of my hand?" Fan Sicong was quick enough to reach out his hand and shouted at Zhong Yi.

"I'm finally up here, and I need to have a look at the backstage."

I turned around and noticed a change come over Zhong Yi's face. She stared stonily at the floor and did not move, her hair hanging from her head, looking as if she was a ghost. The she looked up at me, the face behind her hair turning deadly pale.

"Is what you said true, sir?"

"Nothing but a story."

"But … but look at the floor."

The floor was carpeted with long strips of wood, covered with a red coat of paint, but it was so old that the paint was badly chipped. But there was an area where the paint was almost invisible and the wood was seen, as if it had been scrubbed clean. Starting from the middle of the stage, it went outward, covering more than half of the stage.

"It is so because traces of blood were removed, isn't it?"

"You've been thinking too much, just as you can't help turning your head to see what might be happening behind you when you're told a ghost story at night."

"If someone's throat was slashed here as what happens in your story …"

"Well, I haven't finished my story yet," I interrupted her impatiently. "His head was cut off and taken away in a bag."

Lost in her own analysis of what had happened, Zhong Yi was totally unaware of what I was doing.

All at once she looked up at the ceiling.

"The blood may have spattered up to the ceiling. Yes, look at the dark spots. They must be the remaining bloodstains."

"Don't be silly," Fan Sicong said. "They are stains, but not blood. Don't be misled."

The ceiling was rather high, and it was impossible to have a closer look without the help of a ladder, leaving us wondering what they really were.

"And, and the blood on the floor could be removed, so was the blood beyond the stage. But this log here …"

She took two steps forward and bent over a square-shaped log to examine it closely, while feeling it with her hand.

She stopped at a place and raised her head.

"This part has been sanded with sandpapers," she laughed, her eyes alight with excitement. Her fear vanished promptly.

"Look." She stood up straight, turned to the wall and pointed to the floor. "This is the center line of the area that had been cleaned. Sir, just like what you said, a man was standing right here, his throat was slashed, and his blood spattered all over the place. It was exactly what you have told us."

My expression must have changed to acute embarrassment.

For a moment, I didn't know what to say.

I moved over to the area where blood had been cleaned. It was somewhere behind where Zhong Yi had been, but on the right. I looked up at the ceiling and down at the floor with chipped paint. And then my eyes drifted over to the sanded balustrade.

I felt overwhelmed beyond expression, as if a cricket lurking deep in my heart was being provoked by a goose grass, ready to fight. I smiled silently.

It seemed that someone had been murdered here.

But did it come as a complete surprise to me?

"No one knows where the head is until today." It was a middle-aged tour guide who cut in. She was with a couple, and they came over to enjoy my opera. "It's the first time after so many years it's heard again, from you as a tourist."

"Oh, my God!" Fan Sicong could not help but shout. "It was something that had actually happened?"

Her customers were scared, too, and they asked the similar question.

"Yes, it was. I was right here when the dead body was discovered. You know what, it was a headless, naked body. A corpse sprawled on the stage. I could see the bone sticking out from the cut. I wasn't vomiting, but I did vomit whenever I thought about it when I was back home. I lost five kilos in two months. For a whole year, I avoided this place."

Standing among them, I listened to her, as if I went into a trance-like state of creative writing, which was akin to the feeling when sticky fingers are snaking down your back, when a sharp blade is slashing across your throat, or when a cold corpse from a grave is sucking your private parts.

Although I had talked about the strength of evil, no one had any idea about what I experienced in the writing process, which was full of pain and pleasure.

I turned back and pushed open the door to the backstage.

It was a narrow space like a corridor, jam-packed with old junk—used ropes, long chairs, faded flags, and metal tools such as nails and hammers. There were also several red Chinese lanterns, but they were just skeletons now.

The backstage was nothing more than a deserted small storage, and the old junk had been there for thirty or forty years.

I glanced at the several lanterns before going out.

There was one column log on each side of the stage. "Here?" I looked them for a moment and then asked, pointing to one of them.

The guide squinted at it, for quite a long time.

There was a small hole on the column.

"It may be here," she said. "You know a lot about it."

"What's wrong with it?" Zhong Yi asked.

"A lantern was hanging here that day, a broken one from the backstage storage, the guide said. "It was later taken away by a policeman."

"A lantern?" Zhong Yi asked. "Why was it hung here?"

"I've no idea. What happened here was quite weird."

"No one knows where the head is, so it has been an unsolved case?" I asked.

The guide gave me a peculiar look. "You're right. You know so much about it, but why do you ask? The police even have no idea who the dead man was. I don't think it will be solved after so many years. Where was the head buried? It may have been taken away by a wolf. Of course, if the head is found, the police would know who it was and the murderer may be brought to justice."

With my eyes fixed on the small hole, I was imaging how the broken lantern was swing on the column in an early morning over the stage, where the headless body lay in a pool of blood.

Zhong Yi called me a couple of times, but I ignored her, until she got hold of my arm and began to shake it.

"Sir, you're discussing about the unsolved murder case only to frighten me? You say you know who the murderers are. Do you mean you can break the case?" She looked into my eyes as she spoke. I found the warm gleam in her eyes irresistible.

"Break the case?" I shook my head, smiling. "I know something about the murder case, but as for solving it ..."

I paused for a while and then continued, "The dead man ... his clothes and shoes were taken away, leaving almost no clues for the police. This was an isolated place and it was a rainy night. It's different from a big city, where a murderer could be seen by someone wherever he went. And there would be cameras. He may be careful, but he would leave clues for the police. And ... the killer might cut off the head for a different purpose than to hide his identity."

"You're not being logical enough," Fan Sicong cut in. "The man was stripped to the skin to leave as few clues as possible. Was the head cut off for the same reason? Wasn't it for concealing the man's identity?"

Ignoring what Fan Sicong was saying, I nodded at the guide, smiling. "You see, these people are pretty interested in it. I know little about it, but you know more details."

"Well, well, I have to serve these two tourists." It seemed hard for her to choose.

But the young couple said they would rather listen to her story. I could see the murder case interested them more than the ancient town.

"What do you want to know then?" she asked.

Instead of asking a question immediately, I thought about it for a while before I answered her. "Did it happen in 1995?"

"Yes, it was July 8, 1995, a day I would remember all my life."

The several of them under the stage leaned closer. It was not raining heavily, but Fan Sicong opened his umbrella. Chen Ailing was smoking, and it was the first time I saw her doing it.

As I was standing high on the stage, I felt rather strange when I spoke to them. But I would not be happy to climb down the stage and stand with them in the rain. Anyway, it was a rare chance for me to sense more how vicious the murder on the stage had been.

I was trying to figure out what I would see on the site if I were a policeman.

The lantern!

There were too many to see on there—the headless, naked body and the pool of blood, but I would first set my eyes on the lantern swinging in the wind before I saw the naked body.

As far as I knew, the lantern had caught the eye of the policemen. They should have found some clues in it, but I needed the tourist guide's confirmation.

"They say the cut-off head … was once put in the lantern," she told us.

"Was it because there was blood in it or other human tissues?" I asked.

"I think you're right. It should be the case."

It was far from an accurate answer, but I didn't expect an analysis involving blood type, fractions of bones, and bone marrow. She was not a detective anyway. Comparing what I had already known about the case, her reply was good enough.

"What did the police say about why the head had been taken away from it?"

"You have to go to them for their ideas. But … it's said the murderer feared the dead man would be recognized," she hesitated before she continued. "There're people who believe it was placed in it as witchcraft. When the ceremony was over, it was gone or taken away or even eaten."

What she said left the faces of several people in the group paled with fright.

"Nonsense!" I said.

Probably because of my attitude of supreme indifference, she started to explain, "Didn't you say a moment ago the head was cut off not necessarily to hide the identity? A relative of mine who worked in the county police station told me flesh, human flesh, was also discovered, in addition to the pool of blood. They confirmed it was from the dead man. The headless body was not slashed, so the flesh could only be from the face, which was minced with a knife that it was horribly mangled. It was beyond recognition even when it was left in the lantern. So, it must have been taken away for some other reason. It might be a witchcraft ceremony, but few people in cities know anything about witchcraft and sorcery."

It was not smart to mangle the face of the body to hide the identity. It was already technically possible, even as early as in 1995, to rebuild a face on the basis of facial bones. Of course, the murder might have been ignorant enough not knowing it. Anyway, logically it couldn't be a witchcraft ceremony.

I did not mean to point out her logical error. By asking her a few more questions, I got to know the policemen believed an oil lamp had been used by the murderer because spilled lamp oil had been discovered. He went away with the lamp, along with the murder weapon. But an axe from the backstage was believed to have been used to cut off the head. It had been sharpened on a brick at the base of the stage and was left somewhere before the stage. The fingerprints on the axe had been blurred by the rain water.

"I don't think it had anything to do with witchcraft. But, it was something of a ceremony to not only kill but behead someone. It was sort of a revenge."

"Yes, yes. That relative of mine told me the police had concluded it was a brutal revenge killing."

"Sir, as you're so familiar with the case, I guess you know as well how the police analyzed the motive for the crime." Fan Sicong was trying to be as sarcastic as he could. "You must know things that the police have overlooked. Your work might lead to a settlement of the case."

I flashed him a quick grin before I jumped down the stage. And then I helped Zhong Yi down by almost holding her in my arms. It was an easy job for me to embarrass Fan Sicong.

I stood in the fine rain before the place where the lantern

was, looking up at the emptiness which was once filled with the container.

"That morning, an ugly headless man lay naked on this stage, covered in blood. Almost all his blood had been outside his body, running down the stage. A lantern was hung nearby and in it was mangled human head. Let's say the head was not taken away; it must be in the lantern. Can you imagine what a scene it was and how you feel about it?"

The young lady was so scared that she pressed closer to her boyfriend, making a quavering noise. Chen Ailing appeared calm, but the cigarette between her fingers was about to hurt her. Yuan Ye had a deadpan expression on his face, but he was calmer than anyone else. With his arms folded on his chest, Fan Sicong stared at me, but his feet betrayed him: one of them was pointed to Zhong Yi and the other one took a step backwards out of terror, as if he was ready to escape—you can never pretend otherwise. Zhong Yi's face turned red, with fright and excitement, and I guessed it was when I became interested in her.

"You must be thinking it was brutal, frightening, and shocking, but no one thinks it was weird. Let me tell you why. The scene was a unified, consistent scene." I paused for a while, thinking that I must come across as a psychopath.

"I mean … after it was cut off, the head was put in a lantern, which was then hung up. It was a unified action. To be exact, the murderer became more excited. Brutal revenge killing, and more brutal revenge killing. This is what we call beheading and exposing. He was satisfied by cutting off the head; he had to display it to the public. To protect himself, he disfigured the killed person, but it somewhat dulled his sense of satisfaction as an avenger. He hung it up simply to add to his killing pleasure."

"That was why he exposed it in the lantern? But why did he choose a lantern, not something else?" Zhong Yi asked.

"Simply because lanterns were readily available on the backstage. It's not easy to hang a cut-off head, but people in old times wore long hair, so they did it by tying the hair into a knot.

Of course, there was a different way."

I smiled and restrained myself from explaining what it was. "A lantern was a convenient container, but he might have planned to light it up, so that he could place the lamp on the head. Think about what it looked like when a ghostlike lantern with a human head in it was swing in the wind over the stage and under it was a headless body lying in the rain. What a sight it was in ancient city!"

The crowd remained utterly silent as I spoke, a situation to which I had got used, because I had found few persons congenial to me in my life. But whenever I saw faces flamed with mixed feelings of disgust and embarrassment, I kept wondering in what way they were different from me, as my books enjoy such a large readership.

"But why was it taken away?" a voice asked softly.

The voice reminded me of the several lines of secret codes in *Taking Tiger Mountain by Strategy*, a well-known Peking opera in the Cultural Revolution period: "Why did your face flush with embarrassment?" "I'm full life and energy;" "How come it has grown pale?" "It's waxed because of the cold."

It turned out the woman asked the question was the young lady who snuggled up to her boyfriend. It seemed she was much stronger than she looked, although she pretended to be a sweet and helpless bird.

"As I analyzed it for you, he had put the head in the lantern as a thirstier desire for revenge. But later he changed his mind and took it out. He, as someone who was burning with a desire of revenge, could do this for only one reason."

I glanced around the crowd and continued, "It could not be the cold wind. He chose to kill at that moment, he cut off the head and disfigured the face, he stripped the man to the skin, and he put the head into the lantern. This is something that only a cold-blooded killer does. These people will never salve their conscience or feel frightened for any reason."

It was great to be able to know what everyone in the crowd

had in mind. It was what I felt when I wrote a story.

"Because … because he had a better way?" Finally someone came up with a suggestion, and it was Zhong Yi.

"You're right," I said with a cheerful smile in my eyes.

"I don't think so." It wasn't anyone else but Fan Sicong. "The better way was pleasure, but it would be obvious for anyone to see. Why has the head been missing for years? I have a superficial knowledge of psychology. A killer wouldn't get the extra pleasure from a revenge killing if the head is missing. I think he would have put it in a lantern and hung it up."

"Listen to me. Let's talk about what the better way was first, and then how came the head had been missing. As I said a moment ago, there were often two ways to hang a head up. You all know they could do it by its hair, and they could also put it into a sharp point such as a bamboo pole, a bar or a wooden stick. There was something like this here and it was designed for human heads."

An involuntary cry escaped the guide.

"You mean to say …"

"You're right," I said with a snap of my fingers. "Why don't you show us around?"

We followed the guide through the fine rain. None of us had thought to bring an umbrella except Fan Sicong.

"Jiayuguan was a battle field and beheadings took place from time to time as a public spectacle. It was not surprising at all that they had special places for human heads," I said as we walked along.

"Here we are. Look." The guide pointed with her finger when she was in the protection town.

The Jiayuguan city wall was ten meters high, and it seemed as if we were at the bottom of a well when we were in the protection town. What the tour guide pointed at were several black widgets near the top of the wall, about eight or nine meters from the ground.

"They're iron hooks fixed on the brick wall, for hanging

human heads," the guide told us.

Now all in the group got to know what I had meant, which brought loud or low shocked gasps from them.

"There're more of them on the walls of Jiayuguan," the guide continued. "They're of two types, some facing the outside area of the pass and others the inside area according to the identities of their owners. The outside hooks were for heads to warn enemies and the inside ones for the army and the public."

Her explanation was so professional that I thought none of us was interested in it at this moment.

"Wasn't it more prestigious to hang the head on the hook than to put it in a lantern?"

"Prestigious?"

I smiled, rather friendly, at Fan Sicong. "Right, prestigious. You've got to think like a murderer, feeling what he feels. Of course, you've got to have a twisted mind. This is where you're different from me and where I'm different from the policemen who work on the case. You have those hooks for human heads here in Jiayuguan, so I'm sure the murderer must have thought how foolish he was to work on the lantern before he thought about the hooks."

"But how could a human head be placed on a hook so high? It seems it is not reachable even when you're on the tower over the gate trying to do it downwards," Zhong Yi said.

"You throw it down," the silent Yuan Ye said. "Down about two meters, with the neck towards the point of the hook. With force and accuracy, you can do it."

"As if you're throwing a grenade?" I was trying to joke with him.

Yuan Ye smiled.

"The guy must have tried several times. Then he had to come down to pick it up before he did it. Or he had his own way if he stayed on the top. I'm sure you want to know why the head disappeared the next day. He placed it on the hook, but it couldn't move itself. Or another guy might have been hidden himself nearby and took it away?"

"Right. How could that ever happen?" Fan Sicong asked.

"I have no idea as I was not there myself, but that's where my logic could lead me. This is where it puzzles us, whatever you think the murderer had in mind. So, I guess, the killer himself or herself even didn't know the head would disappear. You know what, what we need is a little imagination, right? That day ... well ... I mean the second day, the day when you saw the body on the stage ..." I turned to the guide, "did it rain?"

"No, it didn't. The rain had stopped."

"When did it stop?"

"I don't know exactly when, but I remember it stopped by sunrise."

I looked up at the sky, but it was too dark for me to see anything. "Do you have vultures around here?"

The guide stared at me for quite a while before giving me a nod. "Yes, yes, we have a lot of them here."

I shrugged. "If it was thrown to the hook, it might not well placed, and it might possibly hang loosely there. Then it would be easy for a big bird like vulture to take it away with its claws. Some fragments of bone from the skull might be lying in a nest somewhere on a towering cliff. As the head had been placed in a lantern for a while before it was taken away, much of the blood must have been there. What's more, it was raining. So there were no clear traces of blood on the ground the next day when it was hung on the wall. It would have been much better if the hooks were checked to see which one was blood-stained. Of course, it can be done anytime, but it would be more complicated. I don't know if the local police can do it with their skills and equipment."

"Well, who was the murderer? Can you identify him or her according to your logic?" Chen Ailing was smoking, one cigarette after another, as if she was a chain smoker who enjoyed her first cigarettes after some effort to give up the habit. She stood away from us, in a place where she could re-examine the whole situation.

"It's impossible," I laughed. "Who do you think I am? There's only one possibility if I can logically tell who and where the murderer is."

I paused, which left them all staring at me.

"That is when … when I myself was the murderer."

I gave them a little bow. "Well, that's my analysis and I hope you liked me as your tour guide today."

Chapter III In Bed

After a simple meal we set out on our journey to Dunhuang. The topic of the headless corpse on the stage dominated the trip. It was none of my business, and I was not at all involved in their conversations, however wild their speculations and creative their imaginations were.

If it was a net and I was already in it, I would have to wait to be caught.

But what should I do when it was not? Or I had been in it for years?

I didn't believe it.

I said no more than ten sentences during the trip. They forgave my eccentricity because of my fame. I had an incalculable, unpredictable disposition, for which they had prepared themselves.

Yuan Ye drove more than fast, and we reached our designation to the best luxury hotel in the city at 11:30 in the evening. It was not too late, as the actual time was two hours ahead of Beijing time, which was used locally. Chen Ailing, who paid for our journey, had a room to herself, and I, as the invited guest, had a single room. Fan Sicong and Yuan Ye shared a twin room, but Zhong Yi lived separately. We were all on the same floor.

"Sir, it seemed you're a bit … restless?" Zhong Yi asked.

It was when I was already in front of my own room.

"Let go of your overused analytical psychology."

In their discussion of psychological states of criminals, Fan Sicong mentioned that Zhong Yi had been a student of psychology. His so-called limited knowledge of the subject was perhaps especially gained to share a "common language" with Zhong Yi, because it was her favorite subject.

"Sir, I thought you were sleeping, and I have never expected you've been listening. Tell you what, I got my certificate of second-class psychological counselor by way of serious exams. It's the highest rank, you know. No first-class rank is granted."

"Great," I said in amazement. I caught sight of Fan Sicong looking back at us over his shoulder near the end of the corridor.

I swiped my card to open the door. "Why not come in for a chat?"

"Great."

I closed the door. "How much do I pay for an hour?"

"Three hundred for you."

"Can I have a discount if you stay with me for the whole night?"

"That's a dirty joke, isn't it?"

"Men have really dirty minds."

"I guess you've something left unsaid—so do women, and all of us have got dirty minds and we act purely on basic instinct. As there are certain times when everyone like us may feel a desire to kill and we're all potential killers, sex is the most fundamental lusty desire."

For a second time, I studied the woman.

"You did it as if you were reading a poem. Now I see you're the best among my regular readers."

"You're absolutely right."

"So it's me who brought about your lusty desire. I should be honored for it?"

Zhong Yi didn't find a place to sit down, talking with me across the bed. I could sense quite strongly that our conversation was becoming rather provocative, an atmosphere which grew heavier with every sentence we spoke.

"You know I did work as a psychological counselor. Three hundred for an hour, and part of it went to the clinic, of course." Looking a bit embarrassed now, she changed the subject and seemed as if she needed a place to sit.

I love women who were challenges to me, but what was always essential for me was that I could defeat them when I was in the mood for it. Well, I knew I was being hypocritical, another original sin.

"I do wish you could be my clinical psychologist. Do you have the white uniform? You would look more like a psychologist with a pair of glasses." I weaved around the bed to where she stood.

"I may need to visit a psychologist, but I know you have a code of practice that actually does not allow you to do it."

Suddenly feeling relaxed enough, she turned up her face slightly. "Why not?"

"Because a counselor isn't allowed to be romantically involved with a client. If it happens, a different counselor is recommended to the client."

"But you're my reader, a regular reader," I said, after seeing her face take on an ashamed and angry expression. "This means you may have pictured many times in your mind what I was like when you had my book in your hand."

Carrot and stick, carrot and stick. It was fun, wasn't it?

She smiled.

"Is what happening between you and me what you have ever imagined?" I asked.

I waited for her to reply. I had been in control of what was going on the minute she entered the room.

It took me by surprise that Zhong Yi got off on it.

The faint aroma from her which had lingered around me suddenly grew wonderfully pungent; it was soft, warm, and sweet. She stepped forward and crushed her mouth onto mine in a lustful kiss. I felt rather strange about the way she was forcing herself on me.

What a woman. I returned her kiss forcefully, while pulling her down on the bed with my arms on her waist.

Quickly we felt an urge to explore, so much as that that we tore our clothes off in a matter of seconds. When her breasts popped out of her purple bra, I could see that the pink nipples were growing harder. I was taken by surprise how her huge tits contrasted with her slim waist, but I didn't have the time to drink in the incredible sight. We wasted no time as we began to thrust ourselves up against each other in an illicit rhythm, our breathing becoming more and more labored. It hurt me as my elbows, knees, groin, and many other hard parts of my body pounded against her. Sparks flew as uncontrollable passion enveloped us and we became soaked in our hot, runny fluids. The sounds we made sounded like a symphony of a surging current, and the two of us, like two notes, were carried along. Oh, yeah, oh, yeah, oh, yeah. The feeling of love that filled our senses was incredible.

When I pushed her off me for the last time, she was already dripping wet with our sweat. I collapsed beside her on the bed, smelling strongly of our fluids and sweat, trying to catch my breath.

When I was beginning to breathe more easily, in rhythm with her, I reached out to caress her up and down. Running my hands up and down the voluptuous curves of her naked body, I was awash with desire again!

Suddenly she moved away from me. With her weight on her arm, she watched my hand travelling on her waist. "Good heavens! You have your gloves on?"

The white silk gloves covered my fingers, palm, and the back of my hand so adequately that it looked like my own skin.

Yes, I didn't peel it off. Is it strange to you? No one has even seen me without my gloves.

I didn't say anything, but kept caressing her.

"It makes me think I'm a dead body," she murmured, lying down again.

"They are different from the gloves used by forensic experts," I whispered into her ear. "They are like a different skin on my hands."

I ran my tongue all over her, from head to toe, drinking in every inch of her body. She was overwhelmed with an urge that came over her, shivering slightly. I finally realized how soft she was. What followed was the normal routine: lucidity, rationality, indulgence, and control. But I somewhat missed the unbridled passion between us we had just experienced.

Our second round of lovemaking lasted much longer than the first one, I guess. I actually had lost track of time in our frantic duel filled with unbridled lust and I had no idea if we had ever groaned and moaned in wild abandonment.

Leaning against the headboard with a cigarette in my mouth, I watched Zhong Yi bending to pick up her bra and putting it easily on her breasts. Her underpants had been thrown to my side, and I reached out for them and handed them over.

"You can stay," I said.

"No," she rejected my suggestion decisively. "Tomorrow ... don't tell Fan Sicong anything."

I smiled.

"You work for an advertising company, but why did you say you're a psychological counselor?"

"I can manage it. I work as a psychologist on the weekends. You know it cost me a lot to become a counselor, and it wasn't easy to get the certificate. A professional psychologist is better paid, and you don't feel like you're under so much pressure."

"I see. Thinking about giving up your job?"

"I suppose so." She had put on all her clothes except the coat, but I was still stark naked. "I've got go."

"Do you know how I learned about the headless body on the stage?"

She looked faintly surprised. I motioned her to be seated and stay longer.

"Are you going to tell me it was you who did it?" She settled herself on an armchair.

I rose, switched on the electric kettle and went for a bath. When I came out, she had two cups of tea ready, waiting for me. I had thought she would be a bit scared, but it seemed she wasn't.

"Maybe I did it. Maybe I was made to believe I did it."

"I thought you would have your gloves on when you took the bath." She watched as I rolled the gloves into a bar as thick as my finger before pressing it into a canvas bag. She reached out her hand, but I avoid her, took out a pair of new gloves from a rectangular plastic case and put it on.

"Where did you get it?"

"I had it made."

"A lot?"

"Yes, a lot," I said, smiling.

"A fetish about cleanliness?"

"A kink." I picked up my jade pendant beside the pillow and put it around my neck. It was carelessly shucked off when we had sex. Putting on my pajamas, I seated myself on the other armchair, with my wallet in my hand. I peeled off three notes and put them under the ashtray, which was beside the clock. It was twenty to two in the early morning.

"Three hundred. Right?"

"You really think so? Well, okay, I'm the only psychologist here. You can only have a different one after we're back in Shanghai."

"I won't need one when I'm back home. Everything would be done or …" I shook my head. "The murder case … in a sense … I knew nothing about it until I jumped onto the stage."

I left something unsaid, waiting for her to ask, but she remained silent. She pulled her leg off of her crossed knees and improved her posture, drawing my attention to—or trying to confirm to herself—I was redefining our relationship differently from a one-night stand. It was a hint that she thought I would get: if I kept up the conversation, it meant that the relation between us would be changed to that of a psychologist and a client.

I accepted. "My idea is it is nothing but a story in a novel. It was presented to me in a weird manner, but I believe it's only a story with fictional characters and plot, and an unreal murder case." I paused, but habitually.

"It seemed to me you're not at all a client who came with the desire to talk," Zhong Yi said. "You've been telling a story, but every sentence of yours is a sentence of suspense."

"Well, professional habit. Everything, once processed in my mind, is automatically arranged in this structural order. It's not bad. It helps you concentrate as a listener. Let me start from the very beginning. It was several days before this journey, two days to be exact, when I saw a hidden fold in my computer. I have to say I myself didn't create this thing, nor had I seen anyone else used my machine. By saying so, I mean to tell you I do have the good habit to scan my computer on a regular basis, but I know almost nothing about the machine, and I don't know how to stop a hacker, if he has the excess to it and something has been tampered with. I'm sure the fold and the files in it were created in this way. I discovered them when I scanned my machine. What a design this was! The hacker must have followed me for a long time, so long a time that he knew well how I used my computer, including when it was scanned for viruses."

"The story in the file is about the murder on the stage?" Zhong Yi asked.

"You're right, but it's a fragment, with no details about the characters and what has happened before and after the case. It's only about the killing. A terrible dark and stormy night, candle flames flickering, sad local opera singing voices coming from afar, a person was beheaded, his clothes stripped and his throat slashed. The description was detailed, vivid, terrible, and graphic."

"It sounds like your own style."

"Yes, it is. And a password was needed for the file, and it was my own birthday. This was a designed conspiracy against me. When I was on the stage and realized the case in the story was actually what had happened and the killer was still to be found, I got to know the scheme was even more devious than I had …" I thought for a while before I smiled. "Actually, it was what I had been expecting."

"I have been wondering what the schemer had in mind. He or she adapted a real case for a story in my writing style, saved a copy of his or her work in my computer and waited for me to read it. It was so happened that I arrived at Jiayuguan, the scene of the crime, two days later. Our journey was decided a month earlier, so I … well … can I ask who planned the route and chose the date of departure?"

"You're … asking me?"

"Yeah."

"You're now a detective, instead of a client?"

Taken by surprise, I shrugged.

"So you prefer to be a client for now."

"Right."

"So you have to be honest with me. My understanding of you, the writer—a sufficient understanding by your stories—tells me, if you're completely sure of yourself, what happened to you would only excite you. How charming it is as a challenge, an opportunity to fight with an opponent who is invisible! But the truth was you had been so anxious and pressured that you came to be as a client. This is unusual, and it tells me you're wondering … wondering if you're the … the writer of the story."

I kept my head low, watching my hands turning from side to side on my lap. Mine were delicate and long-fingered hands, hands of a literary man. They had been work-roughened, but the calluses had gone, barely visible. "You're … probably … right," I said slowly.

She stared at me.

"I have been thinking about the possibility, too." There was a moment's silence before I continued. "Because I had no idea what happened to me in the five years, after all. But the murder took place in the period."

"1995. It was the second year when you lost your memory, and you were still to celebrate your twentieth birthday."

"To be logical, there is always the possibility as long as I fail to remember what happened to me, even though it is a faint possibility, which needs imaginary details to support. That is … I've forgotten that I had killed, or I have chosen to forget about it. But when I write … well, sorry, I should have told you the story was written when I worked on *Old Well, Eyeballs, and Teeth.* For several months, I worked far into the night, and when my imagination got away from me, I saw hundreds and thousands of pictures before my eyes. What I did was to catch some of them and patch them up for a story. To be honest, sometimes I was out of control, like a drunkard. It was possible that I was haunted by the other self, who activated my lost memories, and drafted the story. When it was finished, I was so scared that I put it in a hidden file in my computer. I resumed my normal self and …"

I snapped my fingers, but not as loudly as I had expected, of course.

"The other self was inactivated, and the memories were lost again. I have been led by a virus all the way to this closed door. When it is opened, I would be considered a murderer, a killer who cut heads off and place them high on the city wall. These are all nonsense, of course."

"You've not been frank enough, but you hope our conversation would be helpful to you. You have been thinking about how 'faint' the possibility is, but how come it has troubled you so much if these are nonsense?"

"People tend to imagine the worst."

"But the worst do often happen. Oh, this is not at all a hint, but in your stories terrible things always happen whenever possible, don't they?"

I shook my head, smiling. "I have been caught in a trap of

my own making. I tend to think that way because of those five years. A normal person can never know what it is to lose your memory. It's a frightening gap in your life. It contrasts sharply with your memories before and after it, so sharply that it is always there when you close your eyes. It is a black hole in your life, where nothing exists but everything is possible. I can never stop thinking about what the hell I did in the period. Even my readers are guessing what happened to me. I myself have been much more concerned. When you keep thinking about something, you imagine the worst; you know I have plenty of imagination. Did you ever stare at the ceiling when you woke up at night? You knew there was nothing but a light, but as you fixed your eyes at it long enough the boundaries between the dark parts would begin to twist like a ghost."

"What has helped me as the author of many crime stories? Why are all those killings, graphic details, and hare-brained schemes at my fingertips? I have long been asking myself whether I was born a great writer or what happened in those five years helped me. Yes, these are what you readers of my stories want to know. Is what I can visualize mysteriously when I sit before my computer what we call 'inspiration' or twisted representation of what really happened? It's not right when you say I ask myself such questions every day, but can you imagine what my life is like when I do it every couple of days or even once a week, wondering if I was a murderer?"

"You don't have a dimmest memory of what you did in those five years?" Zhong Yi asked.

"Every text about me says I found myself under a locust tree on the side of the Yulong River. Actually ..." I smiled at her. "Actually it's true, but I left something unsaid. How much you tell others about what has happened and how you tell it often matter a lot. What do you have in mind when you read a passage about me? Do you visualize what I was doing? A young man had awakened from a long sleep under an old tree. Overhead the leaves whispered their drowsy song. He stretched lazily before he sat up. He was dazed, unable to remember what had happened to him. A dreamy, faraway look came over his face. The dream and the years melted under the bright sun, leaving nothing to him."

"What a vivid description from a well-known writer! Yes, it is exactly what I think when I read it. Unfortunately, you can't remember what happened to you."

"Well, when I woke up I found myself badly injured and I thought I was dying. I felt great pain all over. I had head injuries, and I think they were responsible for my loss of memory." I kept my eyes on her. She was listening with great interest, and I noticed how her face changed expression when I talked about my injuries.

"To make it worse, I couldn't cry for help."

"Why?"

"You know why I couldn't."

Knitting her brows in concentration, she spread her hands in a rather exaggerated manner, which meant she didn't know what I was talking about.

I'd forgotten that I was with her as a client. To tell you the truth, I needed everything but a psychiatrist. What trouble it was to act as a patient!

"Because I found myself with this," I said as I took off my jade pendant and handed it over to her.

"Have you ever seen something like this before?"

"Is it Hetian jade? Yes, of course I have."

"Really?" I looked her straight in the eye.

"It's just white jade, not a rare treasure, you know. But I have never seen yours of course."

"No, you haven't."

It was an egg-shaped piece of uncut jade, weighing eight-seven grams and with a brown chain through a hole in the smaller end to make it wearable. The stone was larger than a normal pendant, but it was large enough as something you could play with in your hands.

"It's reported jade in Hetian has been mined for eight thousand years. Jade mining as an industry has a history of about two thousand years. But today even with large and complex pieces of machinery like mechanical diggers, not much jade is produced. Almost nothing is left, you know. The products in the jade market labeled with Hetian as the place of origin are usually made of materials from Russia or Qinghai Province. As they are also from the Kunlun Mountains, they are easily mistaken by amateurs as Hetian products. What's in your hand is more than a piece of Hetian white jade. It's a rare type of suet jade."

"Suet jade?" Zhong Yi said, but she didn't seem at all surprised.

"Yes, it is. Now polished materials or even taluses are considered to be jade pebbles, and stone from Russia and Qinhai are claimed to be Hetian jade. White jade of any type is purposely mistaken as suet jade. But few jade miners have ever seen a piece of suet jade, let alone one as large as this one."

My words prompted Zhong Yi to examine the stone in her hand rather carefully.

"Some jades appear even whiter. But the word 'suet' means much more than 'white.' If you see an animal suet, you would have an idea what suet jade is. Look at it again and you see it looks rather greasy, right? It's greasy not because of my greasy skin; it is naturally so. Also, it looks moist as well. So it's the best stone for jade lovers, even it is not suet. As for the color, some jades are as white as snow, but others may be creamy or greenish. Suet jade is white of course, but it's not icy white—it's creamy. So it looks like the suet taken from around the kidney of a sheep. Tell you what, when it is greasy and creamy, it is suet jade. A piece of suet as big as your fingernail is quite a curiosity. I know a jade expert from a museum in Shanghai, who has a suet pedant around his neck, and he treats it like the apple of his eyes. But strictly speaking, a real suet has one more feature, which helps it enjoy cult status."

Zhong Yi moved to a lighter place to look at it more closely. "You mean this one has the so-called cult status?"

"I woke up with this jade pedant. It was stained pink with blood, but I knew immediately it was something precious. I loved jade, so I quickly went to clean it with the water in a nearby river. I washed it again and again, before I realized that what covered it was not blood. Look carefully and you would see it is glowing slightly pink while it's white in color. It's real suet jade, just like a fresh animal suet."

"Yes, it glows somewhat pink when you look closely."

"You're right. It's not white jade if it's bright pink. I was terribly surprised to see this priceless stone. When I was washing it I realized the river was the Yulong. The people who went out to the town along the river were mainly jade miners. They might rob me of it, you know. For two whole days I traveled along while my injuries tortured me. Finally, I was back to Hetian, although I had a couple of little adventures. To my surprise, I had recovered in the process. Well, what's your idea of my story?"

"I see now why you're so worried," she said, returning my jade to me.

It was a sunken treasure, potentially worth millions of dollars, but she handled it so casually. She simply put it up to the light and looked at it for a while. Obviously, she was not a jade lover. Were all women diamond lovers? Or was it because she was in a professional state of mind so that she acquired a different personality? My personality changed when I wrote. Actually I had been wondering whether I had a different personality in the five years I was lost.

"Yes, how was I wounded? Where did my suet come from? All these puzzles strongly implied something. My life in those five years may be an exacting life, radically different from my writing life now. But so what? Even if I did something special, that doesn't mean I was involved in the murder case on the stage, as Hetian was more than a thousand kilometers away from Jiayuguan. Am I right?"

"But that doesn't mean you were not involved in it, either. Are you asking for my opinion or talking to comfort yourself?" If

I were her, I would have answered in this way, but I didn't know what she had in her mind.

To my surprise, she nodded her head, "Yes."

Well, identities mattered. Why should she as a psychologist have a tit-for-tat talk with her client?

What did she really think about it?

"So, my personal opinion aside, there must be one of two possibilities. The first is that someone may have written the story according to what had happened. Then he or she left a copy in a hidden fold in my machine. It was arranged that I discovered it when I scanned my computer, before I left for Jiayuguan, where I heard about the killing. This was arranged for me to believe I was the murderer. I know this was only the first step, and there must be more coming to me. The second is that I killed and I wrote the story, which I completely forgot about. It happened that the document was infected for me to find it when I did the scanning. And it happened several days later I was where the killing had been carried out years ago. I don't think this was pure coincidence; it must have been perfectly designed by someone who was seeking revenge or someone who loved justice so much that he aimed to show how cruel I was. There must be a series of events, but the murder on the stage was one of them. To conclude, I might be the killer, but I expect similar scenes in the second half of our story, although its beginnings may differ widely."

I smiled at Zhong Yi and then continued, but in a slower pace, "Someone must have designed all this cleverly. Things have been happening, but they are not on schedule. We have to wait for more things to happen before you know if I was the killer. You know what happens in a chess game: one of the two kings has to be placed in check. That's when everything is clear to us."

"But this is not your way. Do you think you'll quietly wait for things to happen?"

"Of course I won't. So I want to know who planned our itinerary, including the time and the route. It so happened that we were in Jiayuguan two days after I found the stories in my computer. Don't tell me this was a strange coincidence. Sorry, I don't mean to interrogate you. We're having a friendly chat, aren't we? You know it's better for me to show it. I don't want to cork it all up."

"That's good," she said. "This is the second time you asked me the same question, and I am honored to tell you how the journey was arranged, sir."

Once again she addressed me as "sir," which showed how unhappy she was about my questions. How unprofessional she was as a psychologist when she was so easily annoyed! Anyway, I was expecting how she would respond.

"We have worked with Mr. Chen for five years, and every year an activity like this is planned. What we do is to invite a celebrity, who helps to promote our products, for a tour with a specific theme. You know, we take photos or do a video shoot. You're with us this time, because I'm one of your readers. As for the route? A couple of my colleagues and I suggested it to our boss, who had the final say. What other routes could be better than this one? You have been writing about the Silk Road, and when you were picked for the team, the route was picked. And when you travel along the Silk Road, Jiayuguan is a must, you know. The date that we picked? Do you still remember I called you about it? You said you could make it in the first half of the month. Then I decided upon the date and I called you again about it."

"Yes, it seems you're right about that."

"But when we left actually wasn't that important, was it? If that … that hacker had been following you he would have learned about our plan two months earlier from the emails between us. And he would have had enough time to finish the story and put it in your computer. If there was this guy having access to your machine, you would be wide open to him or her. You would have no privacy to him or her. Oh, I don't think you have a camera there."

"No, I don't, fortunately."

What the hacker had to do was much more than a story, I thought, but it was enough for him to finish what he had to do in two months.

"It was me who suggested you for the tour. As you're here with the team, I'm part of it. I mean I may be very strongly implicated in it."

I doubled up with laughter, so hard that my sides ached. Straightening up, I moved forward to her, looking into her eyes. I waited for another surge of lust in both of us, longing to bury my face into the crook of her neck to take in her scent. Oh, she hadn't showered yet, so her aroma must be familiar to me.

"No," she raised her head slightly. "I can't find another psychologist for you here and now."

Surprised, I stood back and sat down on the bed.

"Let me tell you what I think about it as a psychologist. Obviously, you didn't stick to the subject whether you killed in the period by talking about who was behind the scheme. This is so because your psychological protection mechanism works, but you may not have felt this self-adjustment. You know, your worries come from the question if you were a killer or, specifically, if you were the killer on the stage in Jiayuguan. You changed the subject of our conversation, but the question has remained unanswered—and it has kept you upset. From the point of mental health, I suggest you come back to the basic question. Technically, it's the same, because whether you killed or not differs logically, when you think about who arranged it, how he managed to trap you, and what he wanted in the end. How can you possibly deal with it properly when you avoid something most basic? Probably you need time to unscramble your thoughts about it or decide what to tell me and what not to. We may have another chat. Shall we make it tomorrow night?"

"You mean tonight?" It was nearly three o'clock now.

She tried to conceal her yawn behind her hand.

I responded with a laugh, "We still have a long way to go for the journey, so it means a lot to you if I was a killer. Am I right?"

"It means a lot to both of us," she said airily. "Ah, yes, does the story say the head was hung on the wall? It was found hanging there."

"No, it doesn't. It's only my own conclusion, when I suppose I myself were the murderer. You know this is something I'm good at."

"But you may be wrong, right? It's impossible for the police to check the hooks one by one."

"Yes, I must be right. If I were the policeman, I would have done so." I looked straight into her eyes.

She looked away.

"Well, let's talk tonight, my psychologist," I suggested.

"I hope you could tell me something I don't know." I had left her visibly upset, but she pretended otherwise.

"I will tell you new things. I forgot to tell you I have more stories."

"Really?"

"In addition to 'In Jiayuguan,' I have another entitled 'In Dunhuang.'"

"Do you mean another murder in Dunhuang?" She stared at me, eyes wide open.

"Yes, another crime story, but we have to wait until tomorrow when we are there before I know weather it tells a true story," I said as I stood up to say good night. "Will you wait? You know I like keeping the audience in suspense, both in my stories and in life."

"A mystical person in a story is always a minor character and dead in the next chapter," she said with a sudden smile as she got to her feet.

"I never do it. You're a woman of eccentric tastes."

The door opened and I wrapped my arms around her waist for a farewell kiss. As I thrust my tongue into her mouth, she was turned on, returning my hold with more passion.

We came fairly close to tumbling into the bed again for another session, as she had partially closed her eyes in anticipation of what was coming next.

"So you have to live a double life," I said.

My words brought her suddenly back to herself, and she stepped away.

"I might tell you tomorrow night that I remembered I was a killer."

I had guessed she would not believe what I said, but I was wrong. Women were more complex animals than criminals.

"'In Jiayuguan' and 'In Dunhuang' are the two stories, but … but do you have another one called 'In Hetian'?" she asked me immediately.

"Yes, you're right."

When I woke up with extensive injuries, I found myself with a priceless piece of suet jade pendant on a chain around my neck. And what had been puzzling me was one of the stories in the fold has the title of "In Hetian," a place known for white jade.

"But I failed in my attempt to open it. I didn't know the password."

If I had been her, I would have said "What a coincidence it was! It was that story whose password failed you." But with a "good night," Zhong Yi turned and walked to the other end of the corridor without looking back.

What a striking figure she cut from behind! The moving ass cheeks were especially sexy. I whistled in my mind before I closed the door and threw myself onto the bed.

I dreamed an erotic dream.

Chapter IV In Dunhuang

Everyone looked strained and weary in the morning, except Yuan Ye. Zhong Yi and I didn't get much sleep the previous night, but did loneliness keep Fan Sicong and Chen Ailing awake? It would be sleazy to keep guessing what they were doing.

Fan Sicong joined me during breakfast and asked airily if I slept well and enjoyed myself. He surely caught sight of Zhong Yi entering my room. He needed to satisfy his curiosity about what we had done together.

What else could a man and woman do when they were left alone?

I felt a sudden impulse to praise his innocence, but I saw Zhong Yi was nearby, watching us. She had told me not to do anything to upset Mr. Fan Sicong.

Had I promised her not to? I remembered I had only smiled without saying a word.

Laughing and joking with Fan Sicong, I removed a long hair on my coat. His face had turned set and hard after.

It was his eagle eyes that were to blame.

A conscientious worker, Yuan Ye gulped down his breakfast and drove the car to the front of the hotel. While waiting for us, he looked at his cell phone. It was something he did often, because the wallpaper was a picture of him with a woman.

Seeing us coming, he put the phone into his pocket.

"Haven't you broken up yet?" I asked.

He darted an angry look at me and got into the car while murmuring something under his breath.

At the same time, I heard Zhong Yi sighing beside us.

I teased her mercilessly for my own good. I needed be in a jovial mood now.

Photographing was not allowed at Mogao Caves, so Fan Sicong could only snap a few pictures beside the pagoda at the entrance. He did it so casually as if he was an ordinary tourist, which I could understand, because I knew he had been absentminded. He had shot with his digital video camera on the car, but only for a short while. As Chen Ailing seemed unworried, I didn't have trouble myself about what he would have in his video clip.

About twenty caves were open for tourists. As there was a guide in each cave for the tourists, I was able to enjoy my free time. Among the five of us, Fan Sicong and Yuan Ye were first-timers in the popular tourist site. But Fan's heart was pulling him elsewhere, and his eyes kept shifting between Zhong Yi and me. Yuan was not showing much interest either. He was here simply because of the famous caves.

We followed the official route for tourists, rushing from one cave to another, along with a big crowd of visitors. Zhong Yi and I walked at the rear. She turned from time to time to look at me, probably wondering where the murder I described in "In Dunhuang" took place. I kept silent, curling my lips into a sneer when the guides talked nonsense.

There was no light in the caves. Each of the guides had a small torch in the hand, pointing with the beam of light to the overhead Flying Apsaras or poorly restored images of the Buddha. A couple of visitors had their own flashlights, too, but they were not strong enough to light the interior up.

"Is this environment an inspiration to you?" I had no idea when Chen Ailing had come over.

"Well, this is an ideal place for a brutal killing. Wow, look at that Apsara; how vivid she is! Oh my God! Her eyeballs look really … ha ha … these things pop up in your mind. Or, when crowds of people come in and out, one of them may be missing. You see a pool of blood coming out from the base of the stature, but the guy is nowhere to be seen."

I was looked on with disapproval before a girl ran frightfully away.

"What do those investigators think about the stuff you write? Reliable? Do they come to you for help for an unsolved case?"

I gave her a sheepish grin. I had been tired of similar questions from my readers.

She stared at me for quite a while, until she realized that I had no intention of answering her question. Shaking her head slightly, she turned to the frescoes.

As a voracious reader of my books, she was expecting my reply. But, as a reserved old woman, she had not told me she loved my stories. I was actually beginning to regret not being friendly to her. I should not have allowed my temperament to get the better of me.

We went from the ground level to upper ones, and then back, to visit the caves for preserving Buddhist sutra, caves where statures had been built and other well-known ones. We ended our visit by appreciating the sitting and lying Buddhas. On our way out, I smiled at Zhong Yi and told her the title of my story was not "In Mogao Caves" but "In Dunhuang." The tourist site was in Dunhuang, which was a large town. She asked if it was on our itinerary or on our way, and I said, "You're more anxious to be there than me."

The car travelled only about two minutes when I pointed outside and suggested that Yuan Ye drive off the road.

"What is it?" Zhong Yi asked.

It was Mingsha Hill. The whole side facing us was pitted with more than a thousand holes of various sizes. A greater part of it was fenced off as a site for tourists and valid tickets were required. The other part was free, and it was the "honeycomb" which I had pointed to. From a distance, it looked like a different site of Mogao Caves, which we had visited.

In front of the cliff was a vast desert land, where no road was available. As ours was a SUV, Yuan Ye chose a slope and drove down it when the vehicle began to rock dangerously.

"Is this part of Mogao Caves? Are we going to it without a ticket?" Fan Sicong wondered.

"You'll know why when we're there," I told him.

The car pulled to a halt at the foot the hill. I jumped down and walked swiftly forward. Not knowing where I was heading, the others followed blindly. It seemed Zhong Yi had sensed what was to come—she was almost trotting beside me. Yuan Ye was in the car, waiting for us to come back.

Like those at Mogao, the caves here were carved into a line of cliffs, which rose abruptly out of the ground. Carved steps could be seen leading to upper levels, but many of them were collapsing, unlike those in the protection zone, where maintenance and repair works were carried out.

The bottom bow of caves was about a meter higher than the desert area. There must be a path of some sort leading to them somewhere in front of us, but I could no longer wait and hauled myself onto it. After a moment of hesitation, I turned to help Zhong Yi up, ignoring the others.

I slowed down my pace and went from one cave to another. All the other colleagues of mine were with us now. I heard Fan Sicong's voice when we had visited a couple of caves.

"Oh dear! There's nothing in these caves. Have they been weathered away into nothing? Why didn't they protect them?"

"They're empty as they were," I said without turning back my head. "They were where the stonecutters lived."

The construction of the Mogao caves is generally thought to have begun in the fourth century, and new caves were added in the following dynasties, until it ceased after the Yuan Dynasty, which fell in 1368. For generations, the stonecutters, stature artists, and painters lived in the caves, spending their whole lives travelling between caves. Behind the magnificent Buddhist sculptural site was hundreds and thousands of heart-rending stories.

I turned specially to Fan Sicong, and he looked deadly pale. He was foolish enough to have sought trouble for himself. It was wrong to do it, man. You're so naive! I thought, imagining how I would pat on his shoulder before he would turn into a column of smoke and wind his way away like a snake.

Very often these weird images raced through my mind. Patients suffering from delusions contrast with artists because they often fail in giving themselves an emotional release.

I saw it just before me.

I could see at a glance this cave contrasted sharply with a dozen of caves we had visited.

The caves for stonemason here were usually smaller with a shallower depth than those at Mogao. The two were different, because the latter were cut for religious Buddha imagines. But the one before me—its entrance was much larger—and it had two rooms.

The room in front of us looked like a cave for a stonecutter, but about one third larger. Toward the back of the room on the left was a smaller room, a long shaped one of about seven to eight square meters. What was special about it was another room built with stone blocks.

As the whole cave was a carved one into the cliff, it was highly unusual to build a room in it. Probably, the room in the room was constructed for a certain new need by partitions of stone walls generations after the cave was completed. It was about the size of a single bed, but it was clearly not a bedroom, but a niche to hold a Buddha statue.

The size of the cave, its two-room structure, and the niche were all symbols of status the owner enjoyed. It must have belonged to someone of the higher social rank or the head of the small community.

I headed directly to the smaller room and looked into it. It was clearly designed so that half of it was in the light from the outside, but the tiny stone-built room was in the dark.

I waited until they all went in and, striking an attitude, I turned around with a pointing finger, until it directed at Chen Ailing, or to be exact, at where her feet were.

"The hand was where your left foot is. A hand cut-off from the body."

They all were frightened by what I had said and stepped back from the place I had pointed to.

It was simply an ordinary piece of rock. Zhong Yi bent to examine it more closely, but she saw no trace of blood on it.

"It was something taking place ages ago," I said, trying to read the expression on each face. "No blood is seen because this was not the first scene. The body had been dismembered before it was carried here when the blood had gone dry."

I moved into the small room.

"It was cut into more than a dozen of chunks, and many parts were left before this small room, but a hand was found at the mouth of the cave and the other in the niche at the back."

I turned on the torch on my telephone to light up the niche.

"It looked like a ceremony of some sort, but how do you explain the handprint on the wall of the niche?"

As I got nearer, with the help of my flashlight I saw a red handprint with the fingers spreading out. It was on the inner wall at a place of the height of an adult.

Shocked, they all came closer.

All of a sudden, I turned the flashlight to their faces.

How interesting to see the expressions were all different!

Dazzled by the strong light in the dark cave, they squinted and turned away. Fan Sicong reacted so sharply that he shouted out.

"What's wrong?" Zhong Yi asked.

"Nothing. I simply want to be alone," I said and went out.

They did not follow me. They must be examining the

handprint more closely.

I sped out to the car, where Yuan Ye was texting, leaning on the door. With a smile on my face, I went up. He deleted what he was writing.

"Oh, I'm sorry. I didn't mean to disturb you. Go on with what you're doing."

He shook his head.

"I don't know what to include in the text message."

He put his phone into his pocket. I thought he had something to tell me, but I waited for a while before he started to speak.

"Those caves are empty caves. What did you see there?" he said. It turned out that he knew all about it.

I smiled.

"Why do you always have your gloves on?"

"It's easier for cranks to be successful, because they stand out from a group."

"Really?" he lifted his hand to his chin. "Well, how do you know we're about to break up?"

"I know about your relationship from this picture you've chosen for your telephone wallpaper. I read the expression on your face when you look at it, and I know how close you're currently."

Involuntarily, he ran his hand over his face.

"It betrayed my emotion."

"But only to me."

I have brought him to the lure. It had never been hard for me to do it.

"Want a brief chat with me?" I asked.

He was hesitating.

"You know what, they say women are unpredictable, but they're less that way than criminals," I plucked out of the air.

Then the coup de grace came: "Maybe I can help."

Yuan Ye then told me all about what had been happening between him and his girlfriend. He must have concluded that this psychotic writer of mystery stories is a nice guy after all.

It was a love story with nothing special. He spoke haltingly when Zhong Yi and others came back. He stopped, but I had already gotten the full picture.

It all happened when he was in the army. He met her in middle school when he was back visiting his family. Distinctly masculine after years of military training, he was naturally attractive to young women and the two fell in love. Unfortunately, as a soldier he could only manage a few days of vacation to be together with her. They kept the relationship going with the help of communication through calling, texting, and messaging each other. When cell phones were not allowed when he was out training or on business, he missed her all the more. Later, she found a job as a secretary of some sort in Wuhan, a large city where she became more exposed to new things. I could sense she must have had a number of casual affairs, but he had always believed in true love. After his retirement early this year, he had been all ready for his marriage to her. He had been with us as the driver to earn money for the ceremony. But she had not accepted his proposal yet, saying she needed more time before she would make a decision. Yuan Ye smelt a rat and he wanted to win her heart by being kind to her, but he did not know how to do it.

Giving him an encouraging pat on the shoulder, I said softly to him before we stepped into the car, "I can certainly be of help."

It felt great to leave someone in suspense.

Once in the vehicle, the two women and the man came over to me for the murder case and the handprint. Fan Sicong said there were a couple of other red marks near the handprint, and he wondered whether the color was from a mineral in the rock and it happened one of the marks was in the form of a human hand. He meant to debate with me, but I answered that there was reason in what he had said, which actually left him disappointed.

Wondering when the murder had happened, Zhong Yi asked me to finish the other half of my analysis. She said it would be great if I could do it in a way as detailed as I had done with what happened on the stage. I had fun telling her that I had forgotten the other part. She mentioned my story "In Dunhuang," but I only smiled to her.

Chen Ailing suggested it could be a ceremony of some illegal cult, because the chunks of the torso were placed along the dividing line in cave, and one of the arms at the entrance and other in the dark recesses. I said she had watched too much of American television series, and she told me there was something similar in *CSI: Crime Scene Investigation*, but it was more like *The X-Files*, as the handprint was found on a rock.

"It doesn't look like something a woman of your age does," I said, laughing loudly. "What a state of mind that you're in your sixties and you love police drama?"

Hardly before I finished, I realized she was the fund supervisor of this journey and I corrected myself by saying it must be her husband and children who loved those dramas.

Caught off guard by many of my tricky questions, she laughed and said she would celebrate her sixtieth birthday in three years.

Finally, no one spoke anymore and an awkward silence followed.

Yuan Ye glanced at me from time to time, eager to know how I could help him.

We had a busy itinerary, mainly because I was unwilling to waste much of my time for a journey only for money. But it had turned out to be quite meaningful. Tonight we would stay in Turban, a small city about 700 kilometers away.

"Which route are you going to take?" I asked Yuan Ye.

"The expressway."

"Why don't we take the national highway first? There's an excellent local chicken restaurant on the side of the highway near Liuyuan."

"Okay. The roads here are not crowded. The highway is just as good as the expressway."

Fan Sicong and Zhong Yi had an idle chat, on and off, which reminded me of what she looked like in bed the previous night.

It had been a long time since I felt physical lust for a woman. I managed to free myself from it to concentrate on the road, so that we would not miss the restaurant.

We almost missed it. At the foot of a hill were three restaurants for drivers and passengers, but the Sichuan and the King of Kings lay empty, with a collapsed wall. We were the only guests in Zhang's Chicken, and we were told to wait for forty minutes, as they have to make everything from scratch. I had the feeling that it would have to be closed in a couple of years. The highway had been used less, as more drivers chose the better expressway. Because no gas stations were nearby, the rest place for drivers would soon be deserted.

While waiting for our dish to come, I told Yuan Ye to send his girlfriend a seemingly wrong text message, which was intentionally written for another woman as a reply to her profession of love. It was a refusal couched in polite words, showing he was not uninterested in the woman at all.

My suggestion surprised Yuan Ye, and he was afraid to do it.

I encouraged him, "Believe me, she would break off your relationship, unless you do something really special to make it work. You know an electric shock to the heart is necessary for a patient at a very critical moment. Human beings are cheap animals. They value whatever others scramble to get. You have to give it up if this doesn't work. If you finally get married, tell her it was my idea when needed and the other woman was simply what I made up."

With that I went to the side of the road, leaving Yuan Ye wondering what to do.

On the other side of the slope was the desert, which stretched for endless miles beyond the mountains to the distant horizon. Open sky, fluffy clouds, vast land, and high wind feature the northwestern region, but it was no longer a magnificent scenery when you were there long enough.

I was not here for the scenery. The person I had been looking for was steps away from me. She was rising from a squatting position, and I spotted her bare bottom and waist and I suddenly realized she had been relieving herself. The whole desert was a large, natural toilet. The place we were at was about two meters lower than the road, making her less visible—of course, when we were at a distance from her.

I walked up. She boomed when she turned at me, with a furious expression on her face.

"You're a ..." she stopped mid-sentence, to voice her anger while saving my blushes.

"Need a place for a nice chat," I told her.

"It was intentional."

I smiled. She headed back, but I didn't move.

"A chat here? My face hurts in the wind."

"How about there?" I pointed in the direction opposite to the highway.

About several hundred meters away from us at the side of a deserted road was a bungalow. With its windows and door wide open, it must have been left empty for years.

The house was quite far from us. Zhong Yi caught sight of me, probably wondering what I had in my mind.

An isolated empty house was a good place for a nice chat, for a man and a woman, who spent the previous night together.

I walked forward and she followed me. Neither of us spoke, listening to the noise of the wind.

We had kept silent until two-thirds of the distance to the bungalow was left before us when she began to tell her story: "I started to read your stories when I was in my second year in the middle school. I asked a boy to borrow some books from the school library for me so I could kill time. He got two from the library. One of them was a love story that I can't remember the name of now, and the other was *Old Well, Eyeballs, and Teeth*, which he had for himself. I was upset and asked him why he thought I read love stories only. So I grabbed the book and, you know what, I began to look for all your stories to read."

"I've read each of your books at least ten times. I never

flick through them. I do close reading, reading for meanings between the lines. I wondered who the author of these amazing books was. When I came across a photo of you, I was surprised. What a handsome guy he is. Of course, as you know, it was only what you were in the eye of a crazy fan. I knew well it was my imagination, but my eyes were glued to you as if you were a big star. Then I vowed to myself that I would never fall in love until I met a guy as cool as you. I even imagined how nice it was if you were my boyfriend. I became even crazier about you when I was in college. Sometimes I thought I was psychologically abnormal. I don't want to tell you all the amusing antics I got up to."

It seemed she was rather embarrassed at the beginning, but soon she looked comfortable and natural, as if she was talking about someone else. She said she did not want to mention those "antics," but she told me some of them—she visited the places in my stories, organized parties for my fans, created a website for my stories, collected different editions of my books, stood in long lines for my signature.

"This is a dream journey for me. You never know how hard I worked to get myself ready mentally, so that I wouldn't make a fool of myself before you."

"It's working so well," I said.

"Really? Even after what happened last night?"

"It's a lovely memory."

Suddenly I realized we were approaching the collapsing house, where three door openings and six window openings were before us. It seemed such a low building even when we were directly in front of it. On a side wall was several words brushed with red paint, but only the word in the middle—expedition—was instantly recognizable.

Suddenly, she spoke much faster.

"I like you so much that I'm simply obsessed with you, unable to live a normal life. Much of the time I hate myself for being so. It's good I've carried out this hope of mine. I don't regret what I did last night. Actually I feel very satisfied. I will always remember last night with you. Yeah, it was good, and one more time would ... you know I won't ruin my life."

We were in front of the door in the middle when she finished.

It would be foolish of me to talk about love. For example, we could begin a serious relationship, instead of enjoying a one-night stand. I was not a ladies' man, and Zhong Yi was the first to have made love to me on her initiative.

In my own stories, a lack of initiative means death.

"And now, what do you want to tell me? Or shall we return?" she asked, standing in front of the house. "I'm starving."

I didn't answer her right away. The surviving red words read "... sland Expedition Ti ..." and under it were several words in lighter color—"Kunlun Tiro," which must have been a jade store.

My eyes drifted over to Zhong Yi's face.

"Would you like it if I do it with you without my gloves on?" I looked at her, grinning from ear-to-ear.

Her mouth suddenly set in a determined line.

"It would be difficult for me to get hard without my gloves on. Sorry I'm only joking!"

Zhong Yi allowed herself a wry smile.

"Why don't we go in?" I said.

I knew it was everything but a jade store. No one would even think of having a jade store in the uninhabited place, unless he intended to invite robbers. Most probably it would be a restaurant or a garage. The "Kunlun Tiro" should be "Kunlun Tire," because the last letter had been stained and last word in the above line should also be "Tire." It used to be repair shop.

After a moment's hesitation, she followed on.

It was an empty house, and the paint was peeling from the gray walls. The floor was covered in a layer of fine sand, and I left clear footprints behind me. I was examining one of them when Zhong Yi came in.

I moved my foot on it from side to side, and the color of the floor began to show.

I continued and more of the floor was exposed. A broom

would have been more effective, but soon we could see blood on it.

As the floor was heavily bloodstained, the traces of blood probably had not been removed. It was a reasonable guess, because water was not readily available as the house had no piped water.

Zhong Yi saw it, too. "Well … is this what you have in 'In Dunhuang'?" she asked softly.

"Yes, it is. Dunhuang has more than Mogao Caves."

"What about what had happened earlier?"

I shook my head in silence. It was what I had intended, but I didn't want to explain.

Her telephone rang. Taking a glance at it, she said, "It's them. Shall I ask them to come over?"

I shrugged, meaning it all depended on her.

I was walking around a post outside when they came. As the years passed by, the clues at the scene of the crime had faded into the background. Unlike the case in Jiayuguan, for which the woman guide could recount important details about it, this one was almost clueless. But the blood in the room, the post and the surrounding led me to believe what described in the story of "In Dunhuang" was a real story, just like the one in "In Jiayuguan."

"I had expected to learn from you about the West, but it has turned out to be a journey about crimes," Chen Ailing said.

"Well, you've guessed at the truth? But Zhong Yi hasn't, from what she talked about over the phone." I flashed her a smile.

"The opera stage, the caves, and this empty house … if I haven't felt a thing I would be too … well, well, are you sure you recommended the highway for the chicken restaurant? Give us the full picture—it would be a torture if you bog down in the middle, as you did when we were in the caves."

"You said it. Don't keep us in suspense."

I could tell Fan Sicong was being ironic, but rather indirectly, which was what I had expected.

Now the only person who I found hard to deal with was Chen Ailing.

"Good. I'll tell you all I know about it. What happened here was, to some extent, more appealing to me than the murder on the stage."

"Do you mean it was more cold-blooded and more brutal?" Zhong Yi asked.

"Death helps everything to be what they really are. However cold-blooded, brutal or psychotic it is, well, it's what it is, naked and real."

My philosophy of life left them standing there staring. With a faint smile, I continued, "Uh huh, you're right—it was more cold-blooded and brutal. It's something I like."

"A winter night, snowless, rainless, but windy. The guy was driving, but people who had seen his car are all dead now."

I started to recount the story of "In Dunhuang."

I was thinking the story was not an eyewitness account, just as "In Jiayuguan." The writer must have interviewed some local people or read a police report and pieced together the fragments with his own imagination.

When I narrated, I tried to screen out what the writer had added to it, so that the true story was left. It was not something hard for a mystery writer. I could tell at a glance what was original and what was fictional.

Or could I really do it? I suddenly asked myself involuntarily. Then I gave an amused laugh as I found my question quite absurd.

"Why are you smiling?" Zhong Yi asked. "It's a weird smile on your face."

I waved my hand and turned off my smile, before I continued with my account of what had happened that night.

No one knew anything about the vehicle, but it was a car. On a late night in a place as remote as this one, the breakdown of one's car was the best excuse to wake up a garage owner. It might be true the car broke down and he was not cheating.

There were three living things there: a female dog and the father with his daughter.

The dog was not chained, as they usually were at night in the place. But she sensed danger and started to bark loudly at the car owner, so her master tied her to a post.

She was the first to die.

Her throat was slashed. It was when the car was nearly fixed and the animal was howling. The chain was stretched tight and the guy squatted on the ground before her in a place just beyond her reach. With a swoop of his knife, she was killed instantaneously and her noise was no longer heard. Nothing special was later discovered on the dog's teeth and claws, which meant no clues about the killing had been left. It was a brutal, experienced killer. He had to be sober enough to do it so neatly, although the dog was fastened.

The next one to die was the father. Hearing no noise from his dog, he went over to see what was happening. He even asked "What's wrong with the dog?" Oh, no, no, if I were the guy … yes … it was the daughter who came over, as the father was working on the car. But she was held hostage, which meant her father was under his control.

The father was then called over for an exchange with his daughter. He may be blustering: "Hi, man, what're you doing? I will give you whatever you want." Before he finished, he was stabbed in the chest and became powerless to fight back, but he would not die immediately. The father and his daughter were then tied up in a room, where the father's blood is still visible. After he started a fire, the guy dragged them out.

The highway before the chicken restaurant was already used as the main road at the time, and the one in front of the repair shop was usually avoided by drivers, especially at night, but a few of them did choose it. The driver who the police interviewed three days later said he had seen light from the back of the house, thinking it was from a wood fire. He had also heard whimpering cries muffled by the wind, which was so frightening that he pressed the accelerator harder. He had caught a glimpse of a car at the back of the building. To be exact, it was an indistinct shape of a car in the fire light. He did not have the time to see what car it was; either was he brave enough to do it.

The cries were from the two victims. With rags in their mouths, they could only whimper, however desperate they were.

It was wise that the driver passed without stopping to see what was happening by the fire. When the police arrived the following day, they had had the impression that the scene must have been visited by wolves, which used their super-efficient sense of smell to find food. The police were right, but it was later confirmed that the wolves were not alone in dismembering the body.

The fire was burning. The father lay on the ground, with his arms and legs securely tied, bleeding heavily from his wound. He was dying, and he felt the world was becoming colder and was going away from him. But the terrible pain he was suffering sobered him up a little.

The guy started to cut his flesh, chunk by chunk.

I noticed Chen Ailing was smoking again. It was the second time she did it in these days.

She was the only person whose eyes were not on me. She looked down at the ground, as if she was listening to me or thinking about something else.

Of course, she was listening, I thought. Nothing could distract anyone at the moment, unless she knew already what had happened.

How vicious it was to cut into the flesh of a father before his daughter.

The guy was skillful enough so that the father did not die too soon. He even put the flesh on the fire.

I would not be shocked even if a guy as brutal as him put the flesh into his mouth.

The bones in the victim's chest, back and thigh were finally seen. He was reduced to a skeleton the next day after the wolves ripped the rest of the flesh off.

Probably because the killer had got carried away in the game of killing, the daughter managed to escape into the desert with her life. Finally, she came to the highway for help.

She did not survive too long. It was dangerous to hitchhike on a road in a dark night; no drivers were brave enough to stop. It was hard for the police to know exactly which vehicle ran her down. It was possible that many cars and trucks had driven over her body. When the next day dawned and a car finally stopped before her, it had been run over so many times that it had been no longer in the shape of a human body.

"I don't think you're interested in the details about how the body was split … how many cuts and how many chunks. I will omit all unnecessary details. So this is what I know about the case. It's still to be solved, just like the one happened on the stage in Jiayuguan. One of the difficulties for both has been the motives for wanting the victims dead. Evidence might show the murder in Jiayuguan was committed to revenge, but it seemed so far that this one, which was more brutal, took place for nothing."

"You mean the police have failed in establishing a motive for it? So have you?" Chen Ailing asked, much to my surprise.

"I mean the policemen." I smiled, looking her in the eye. The look in her eyes was a mixture of worry and hope, which contrasted sharply with the mere curiosity in the other eyes.

Is she expecting that I could solve the case? How interesting!

"Death has its own peculiar enchantment. Life is the most curious experience, which has two finest moments—the moments of birth and death. Every one of us is filled with joy when a baby is born, but few of us have the courage to face the beauty of death, the exotic flower of evil. Why are so many people mad about murder stories? Because they are an indirect but safe means to resist the seductions of death. To face it is too dangerous and a heart of stone is needed. Of course, it generally means an extremely abnormal state of mind. So, most murderers need some pragmatic reason to kill—for love, wealth, or whatever. But, for a small number of people, death itself is the reason, or the motive. A good example is you swallow when you see tasty food. It's not because you're hungry, but you want to eat it."

"Do you mean that a murderer's motive can be simply to murder, because they love to kill?"

"Yes, you're right. Actually, I've written about similar cases. These are the most difficult cases for detectives, because such murderers kill simply because they're interested in killing. They get immense pleasure out of it. Don't you think this case of murder is a good example? All the signs point to a spur of a moment. It might be the daughter, the dog, the moon over his head, or even an image popped up in his mind that triggered his desire to kill. And he went for it. I don't mean that he was without motive or he loved to kill because he was still at large or because we don't know yet what his reason was. What he did afterwards was also what a murderer who enjoyed killing often did."

Chen Ailing took long pulls on her cigarette. She then turned her head to me and looked me up and down.

"These killers are all extra calm. Their wire-like nerves allow them to travel between dangers with remarkable mental resilience and enjoy the pleasure to kill. The guy in this case caught the two victims by killing the dog first and then taking the daughter hostage. He parked his car in a hiding place so that it was not to be seen. It means he didn't ignore passing vehicles on the road, but he chose to kill in the open and unduly prolonged the process. Was it something hard to understand? No, it was his psychology. He was quite sure no one would park his or her car and go around to the back of the house to see who was making a fire and, at the same, he was all ready to shoot at anyone who would pop up before him. The potential danger of 'being seen' caused through him a surge of pure adrenalin, which he enjoyed immensely. As I said just now, he was traveling from danger to danger and dancing in a minefield. But, this was the first of his seasoning."

Thinking about how psychotic the murderer was, I could not help swallowing. I had published numerous stories of vicious crimes, but it seemed life was always my teacher.

"The second seasoning was to torture the father to death before the eyes of his daughter. The father got held because he wanted to save his daughter, who stayed because of her father. I was not an eyewitness, but I've been doubly sure it was an environment he created intentionally. It was a difficult dilemma for both victims, but it was a source of tension for the killer. These were the seasonings, but what was the main course? A prolonged process of dismembering of the body! It was something a guy who enjoyed the process itself chose to do."

Fan Sicong's face blanched in terror. "You're using seasoning and main course as metaphors."

"It makes you sick? Or I'm being too cruel? Which do you mean? A detective is a great detective only when he thinks the way criminals think. It's also what makes a mystery writer a great writer. Of course, ordinary people like you eat eggs, but they never care about what the hen looks like. When eggs are mentioned, I feel hungry now. Shall we go back? It's time to enjoy the local chicken."

Silence reined the short journey across the desert, and the only sound I could hear was the roar of the wind. "I have the feeling that you were holding something back," Zhong Yi said when we were approaching the highway.

I began to chuckle, but my laughter quickly died away in the wind. I saw Fan Sicong, who was ahead of me, jerking his head. It was a great day for me, but others might be wondering how weird I was.

"You know me well, indeed. It's hard for me not to speak it out. Actually, I have a somewhat different idea about how it might have ended. What I have told about is the official conclusion from the local police."

They all stopped to look at me.

"Sometimes, I find it hard to understand why investigators who deal with crimes everyday could often be wrong. The death of the daughter tells us how experienced the murderer was in this trade. Nobody is born that way, even if he is so talented."

Hearing the word "talented," all the faces before me twitched.

"However talented he is, several lives must have been lost in his hand before he became so experienced. These guys were self-processed and sober, and the experience allowed him not to make any careless mistakes. So it's hard to imagine how the girl could escape from him and mowed down on the road."

"You mean she was not knocked down and killed?" Chen Ailing asked.

"She was, but it was not by a car. Neither did it happen on that road. Let's follow the logic of what we were saying: what could the murderer do with the daughter after her father had been killed? To stab her death with a knife? No, no. It would be too easy for him, and it would not be fun. He would want it to be more exciting, but it's hard to know what other tricks he would choose to play. The police have concluded that she was killed by a car and let me suppose their medical experts are right, then I would say the guy must have let her go before his car drove over her. He kindled a spark of life within her and snuffed it out, which is a game many killers are made with. Let's imagine what had happened: the girl's legs were so weak that she could hardly stand, but she was given the chance. The car was beginning to roar behind her, and she was dazzled by the high beams. She took faltering steps and struggled along. He went slow and followed her until she finally collapsed when his foot jammed against the accelerator."

It was a graphic account, as I simply spoke out what popped up in my mind about what may have happened. I was thinking how lurid it had been if I was the killer—perverted with tension, brutal with beauty.

"I was wondering why he fabricated evidence by moving the

body to another road?" Zhong Yi was the first who had recovered from the daze.

"I guess that he must have realized at that moment what he had done might betray him as the murderer. It would be a tell-tale clue if he had left the body where it had been. Of course, the police had to be sensitive enough."

"A clue?"

All of them, including Yuan Ye, frowned at me, wondering what the clue was.

"Forget about it. It's food time. I guess the daughter may have been killed on the road before the garage. When you fall prey to panic, you make mistakes. Among the hundreds of choices available, she must have chosen the worst by belting down the road. But the crazed killer must have considered all the possibilities before he acted, to make sure she would be dead. You didn't expect this analysis of mine, did you?"

Silence, nodding, and shrugging.

"I mean, the killer would have thought the possibility that the victim would fall off the road and run into the desert. If the policeman thought the same, he would be able to come to the conclusion that the killer drove a car."

"Oh, you're right."

"So the killer made a lengthy detour to leave the body on a different road. It was run over by hundreds of vehicles that night. This is a crack, but it has been well covered up."

"But you've discovered it," Chen Ailing said while blowing smoke rings.

"It makes no difference, because the police have missed it."

"It would have made a difference, if you have been among them."

"Yes, that's true, but how could that be? Just like what happened on the stage, the murderer would be at large, even we know who did it, because it happened so long ago. I'm even fairly sure the car was easily identified as it was a rarely seen type of SUV. This was the reason why the driver put much thought into covering it up. When the murderer is known to be someone travelling alone in Xinjiang in an expensive car, he would be like a rat in a trap when all the controls are guarded. He was a guy who wouldn't take two lost lives seriously, and he would kill more. So he wouldn't even think of changing his itinerary, as if nothing had happened."

There were some audible sighs around me.

"Enough," I said. "Shall we go for some food? I'm half starved."

"How come you still have an appetite?" Similar deep sighs were heard again.

Chapter V A Jigsaw Puzzle

"Have you ever given thought of me as the murderer?"

"No, never," Zhong Yi said.

"You're not telling the truth," I challenged her.

The room was just like the one we were in last night, but smaller and newer. Between she and me was also a small tea table, but she was sitting in an armchair catty-cornered before mine across it, while we sat shoulder to shoulder the previous night. The change meant a change in the way we should communicate with each other.

Of course, a more marked change was the sheets on the bed were not at all crumpled.

She simply smiled at what I had said.

"It's rather cold." She rose to turn off the air conditioner.

I thought she was not yet a qualified psychological consultant, who would have exerted all herself to let me know she was on my side, with a look of disbelief on her face that I had to do with the murder—to provide an environment as friendly as possible for us.

Actually, I would never believe her, however she would feign trust in me. Neither would I feel uncomfortable and refuse to cooperate in the conversation to come. In this respect, her silence of assent indicated how well she knew me.

"You've been quiet since the dinner," she said, resuming her seat.

"I'm a quiet man."

She expected me to continue.

"I am thinking about if I was the murderer."

I took a little sip of my tea. It was no longer hot. Noisily, I placed the cover on the teacup, either because I had not been careful or because my hand had trembled.

It seemed she had sensed nothing about it—she looked at me calmly, almost with an air of placidity.

"Great writers are persons of many talents. One of them is they have implicit faith in the world they portray. They can even see, hear, smell or touch what's happening there. They lead a double life, travelling from one world to the other. I often visualize what is happening in the imaginary world, and I make parts of it into my stories, leaving the rest in the unexpected depth of my memory. Sometimes I talk with the people, some of whom are alive and others are not. I always believe it's a talent of mine."

I swallowed, as if my throat had gone unbearably dry and the tea I had sipped had been of no help at all.

"The images of the opera stage in the rain, together with the iron hook on the wall, bare but as if with a head on it, and the deserted house in the remote desert, niggle away in my mind. They're twisted but truly realistic. Shadowy figures nearby or far away, dancing flames, snake-like trickles of spreading blood, smell of blood in the wind. I feel I am travelling through time, connected telepathically with the murderer to see with his eyes and to feel with his heart. Sometimes it is a picture unfolding before me, but sometimes those images overlap to form a box filled with compressed noises and me."

Turning my head to her, I saw Zhong Yi was listening intently. She was already pulled into the illusion I had created.

"I always believe it's a talent of mine, when some factors in my blood are motivated. I even wondered if I was a serial killer in my previous life, but I've never expected I could be a killer myself. But I'm thinking about it now, and I can't help doing it.

A voice is echoing in my ears, telling me what I often visualize has nothing to do with any scene of crime—they're nothing but a mixture of clues of various murder cases and my imagination. They're part of my memory … my memory … you know … my memory. They were all dead and buried, but they've come to life again, rising from the graves with their waving hands in the air."

A loud laugh escaped me. Even I myself felt my voice was very weird.

"Why didn't I ever, at the very beginning, think about the possibility I myself could be a murderer? As I have no idea about what happened to me in the five years, I'm a writer of genius in crimes of murder and murder psychology, and fictionalized stories in my own style about brutal killings that has confirmed to have really happened were found in my computer, it would completely defy logic for me to deny any involvement in them. I've never thought about it, which, as I consider it now, is what we call inverse thinking, against the way I do things. So the only explanation is I have kept an innermost secret, but subconsciously. In other words, there is another hidden self of me."

"Well, my books are becoming popular. Does it mean those dim memories are coming flooding back? A real murderer, a cold-blooded serial killer, has been sitting in his study to write about what he did in the past?" I asked Zhong Yi, rather unexpectedly.

Zhong Yi managed to restrain herself, but she went rather pale.

I started to chuckle. Was it the other self of me? I forced myself to calm down, so that I looked natural and normal, fearing Zhong Yi would be frightened away.

"Whatever these speculations mean and however frightening they are, I think I should be as objective as I can. I've got to face the challenge, whatever it means to me in the end. Hope you can be of help. I need someone to tell me when I go astray. Oh, well, I see you're frightened, which is natural enough. Let me know when you don't want to."

The room was then filled with a deathly silence.

I waited for a few minutes before I drank my tea again. It seemed that Zhong Yi was activated by the noise made by the teacup and its cover, which helped her make her decision.

"Do you know what it means to you, a well-known writer, if it is found that you were a killer?"

"A great scandal," I shrugged. "That's all."

"To the millions of your regular readers, it would be a disaster. It would shake their beliefs and change their views of life. Readers of crime stories often gain power from acts of cruelty in the books, and they read about death to live a better life. But you ... you have been their hero, their godfather who is full of evil ideas. Many of them would crack without you. Are you going to do it?"

"Crack?" I could hardly hide my smile, "Nonsense. Where do those symbols and meanings come from? It's nothing but a scandal, and it is significant only because it makes a terrific conversation piece. And possibly something more—if I am a murderer, I will write my last story before I'm killed. It will be the best of all my books, and those fans who will came near to a breakdown, as you said just now, and those who are so self-righteous that they sniff at my books will be more than a little interested in it. I bet it will sell ten times better than any of my stories. Oh, no, it will be banned in this country, I'm sorry."

"These are your words at long last. What you said earlier sounded like a different person." Zhong Yi was no longer nervous. Her psychological adjustment ability was much better than I had expected.

"I understand you're about to search your memory. I'm glad you trust me, making it possible for me to know what happened to you in the mysterious years. It's something all your readers are crazy about. But I've got a question to ask you."

"Go ahead."

"Well, all successful mystery writers show us in their books the ugly dark side of life such as violence and twisted minds. They see the world differently from ordinary people, but it does not mean they tend to kill or they have killed. About the stories in your computer, I agree with you that it was a trap set for you. I was shocked to learn that the stories are about what really happened, but it's too early to say you were the murderer before we know how they were put into your machine at the right time. You know this, and you talked about it with me."

Stiffening her back to sit bolt upright, she looks into my eyes. "But you've changed your idea. You must have good reasons to reverse your earlier judgment, which seems to be independent and objective. Now you're wondering if you ever killed. You said you need my help, so let me know what your reasons for the change."

Reasons?

Did I have them?

To be honest, I didn't know how to answer her. How should I answer her? I liked people who were intelligent, but they could always be an unexpected trouble.

A lie requires a greater lie to be believable. Now I had to make up a wonderful story for what I had made up about my self-doubt as a murderer. What a trouble I had asked for myself!

I wouldn't mind calling white black, but it was much more difficult to explain why it was black. I had not been involved in the murder of the garage owner and his daughter; neither had I anything to do with the human head on the city wall. The stories in my computer were accounts of what had really happened, but they were not my work. I had been pretending otherwise, and I really did not know how to make it all up.

I had not expected Zhong Yi to have taken it so seriously. If she was an ordinary reader of my stories, she would have been intensely curious about the rumor that I, a writer she loved so much, had killed. When I had indicated that I might have been involved in it, she would have been all the more so while appearing remarkably calm. If she had some underlying motives, she must be the one who had been trying to trap me, leading me to believe that I was responsible for the murders. Now that I had changed my mind, I was an animal walking right into her trap, at which she must have secretly delighted and become even more cooperative.

Was it possible that she had nothing to do with it, and she, as a secret admirer of mine, was simply unwilling to see me as a killer because she considered me as a hero? Or was she working as a great consultant psychologist, to study me thoroughly and thoughtfully so that she would not miss any detail?

I did not have the time to think about it; I needed to reply to her, telling her what the "reasons" were.

"Yes … uh … it was because the death of the daughter and the head on the hook. Those details not included in the story or different from what is said in the story all of a sudden raced through my mind. There was logic behind what I have told you about them—it seemed I came to a conclusion after a coherent process of analysis, but they came to me out of nowhere, but as if they should. It all happened in a way like I knew well how it took place. You know what I mean."

Zhong Yi frowned, with looks of utter disbelief on her face at what I had made up.

"Most of the time, there's underlying logic behind an idea that has popped up into your head," she said. "It's often the case you understand the logic by considering the answer, which come to you first. You know what, sometimes your brain begins to work by itself before it receives your instruction. It happens very often when you constantly repeat what you do."

"And if you killed and wrote about them, how could you left us confused and even make mistakes?" she continued.

I had a ready answer to this question of hers.

"I might have done the work in an abnormal state of mind and, as a result, I left something out or made mistakes. I may be another self of me or another personality. I had no idea what he was doing or what he had in mind. It may also be the case I killed but the stories were not mine but written by a different guy, who knew the cases well or who committed a different crime to revenge and he knew I had killed. If she was the murderer, she would know only the crime in which she was involved, so she had to guess other details for the stories. This may be why they don't give full pictures."

I watched the expression on Zhong Yi's face when I said the word "revenge," but it betrayed nothing of her thoughts. She looked self-absorbed and deep in thought, but with a doubtful air on her face. The word had made no impact on her.

"No matter what, those images popped up into your head, as you said, can be interpreted by the theory of subconscious, and they're not hard evidence, but …"

Shaking my head slightly, I pointed with my finger at the place where my heart was. "It has made me less confident. You know, there's no logic as to what confidence is. I had never troubled about the question if I could have ever killed, for no reason at all. If things are all logical and rational, there would be no miracle in the world and no evil, no heaven and hell. We're all entirely free in it. As a matter of fact, humanity lies in desire, instead of the so-called logic. This works better than any other evidence. I now believe I killed in those five years."

I spoke the words as my shield and buckler, primarily to confuse. I remembered telling her last night I had suspected myself as a murder whenever I thought about "my lost life in the five years." It indicated I had not been that confident, which was contradictory to my theory of confidence. As I had drawn a line a moment ago between confidence and logic, she would not think more about it. I have chopped and changed so much … like a teenager who was struggling between showing and not showing his puppy love. But, to help my statements add up in such a short time, I had no other alternatives but to trash myself.

"But I think you said you were a murderer … it needs an impartial analysis."

I shrugged and spread my hands. "That is where you're needed."

"I guess I'm nothing but a psychologist."

"It makes no difference. Well, I mean ... I hope they're the same."

Zhong Yi stared at me in disbelief.

"It'll be nice if your self-doubt is finally proved to be nothing but what you've imagined. I don't think I'm more than a psychologist—a detective, a judge, and a victim," she said with a smile on her face.

"Whatever I did in the five years, I'm a different person now. If I'm a man with dual personality, you've got to be careful not to invite the other side of me. This is a real test of your mettle, Miss Psychologist."

"Oh, well. As you're talking about confidence and being illogical, shall we put aside the question who wrote the stories, which is rather logical?"

She slowed down, her voice becoming softer and gentler.

"You don't remember well what happened in those five years, but I think some vague images and sounds from it would come back to you occasionally, whatever fragments they are. These nuggets of information must be unique. Can you tell me what your feeling is when you think about that period in your life? Tell me in one sentence, or a word."

Those five years?

I had never had the idea to describe my life in the period of five years in one word. When I thought about it, a word popped into my mind: intense.

Intense pleasure and intense pain, in the wilderness, among rocks, at white beaches, in dense forests. Only the intense could express the sweets and bitters of life that I had tasted.

I had never been afraid of recalling my life in the period, including the lurid details of the intensity. That was a fertile source of ideas not only for my books, but for the life I was living now. I had a much better understanding about life and death.

Instead, the five years had become a sacred site in my mind, which I visited from time to time. The hazy and episodic memories, as a result of my own fault, kept coming to me and flying around me. They sometimes hung in the air before or behind me. I could absent-mindedly get hold of a piece and play with it for quite a while before I let it go. Was it a contradiction to my visit to it? No, not at all. Like Saturn's rings, it had a beauty of enigmatic quality. But when you dived right in it, you would land on a piece of debris, which turned out to be cold and coarse rock or ice.

As it was happening to me now, some debris was popping into my mind: beautiful jade in a palm, a work-roughened hand with the jade, a flash of pure white. As they were stretching to form a whole episode, I rubbed my nose and a sharp pain shot through my head. Instantly, they vanished.

What should my answer to Zhong Yi's question? Of course, I could never tell her the truth. Intense? Her questions would follow, because intensity meant clarity, details, and happiness symbolic of life and death. If it is something intense one feels about one's experience, how is it possible he remembers nothing about it? Instead, it should be something he always remembers. I had to be careful before Zhong Yi, rather than ask trouble for myself.

To continue to play the game about the five years with her, I could only reply her with vague words that could be variously interpreted.

"Eyes closed."

"What?"

"It's something when you close your eyes. It's not pitch darkness. You can see many bright spots that move randomly. They form various patterns, which can be figures of some people. But they all break up at the last moment. Yes, it's something when you close your eyes."

"How does it feel when your 'eyes are closed' and the spots appear and move? Calm? Passionate?"

"A wistful longing for the past and a strong feeling of affection. That's it."

As she talked to me, Zhong Yi scribbled in a notebook, probably for later use for her analysis. In doing so, she lowered her head from time to time, naturally avoiding my eyes. Now I was wondering whether she had a scornful look on her face, or a thoughtful one, or a look of disgust, but she put her face down again.

"Not terribly excited, say, frightened or irritated? If it's a wistful longing or feeling of affection, it means that period of your life was filled with a sense of well-being."

Her subtext seemed to be I would not have killed in a happy time of my life, but she was only pretending. She did it simply to help me to relax my vigilance. If I were her, I would be doing the same—make believe that I was on her side, so that she could become less defensive. I would hold back from a final confrontation until I felt quite certain of success.

Was it my way to treat others? Yes, it was.

Self-confidence is not at all a synonym of arrogance. I should remind myself from time to time, on the long journey involving murder crimes, about the differences between the two. Whoever among them was the killer, I knew well now what a challenge he or she was for me. I even could not afford to ignore Fan Sicong and Yuan Ye, who looked stupid enough. Actually, they would be more dangerous when the murderer was one of them—they were great actors!

One of the four—Chen Ailing, Fan Sicong, Yuan Ye, or Zhong Yi—must be a murderer. I didn't mean he or she had killed, but would kill ... me.

I had long been sure about it, even at the very beginning of the journey.

How great I was in the best of spirits now!

I grinned and began to talk about something about my "happy period" to satisfy Zhong Yi's expectations.

Wind with the smell of grass, strong current in the Yulong River, unsteady sound of bells were more materials, which could be woven together with a little imagination, than episodes of memories.

Zhong Yi was solving a jigsaw puzzle by joining dots and

lines up to complete a drawing, before she made up a life story of a teenage who ran away from home for love.

"The girl with soft, white skin was your close companion. When you talked about her from your fragmented memory, it seemed you were a different person. If it had to do with the seasons such as spring and winter, you must have been together for quite a long time. And, you mentioned a locust, a tree that was seen everywhere in the region. As there was only one of them in front of your house, the one you mentioned must be among the two that you remembered best, the other one being the tree you saw when you woke up. You talked about the tree when you talked about the girl, so she must be somewhere near the tree in an episode. In other words, she must have passed the gate of your house, before you left. So, it was because of the girl that you ran away from home."

"I'd rather say I left school because of my poor grades," I said.

"Probably both worked. Just now, you talked about jade, Hetian jade, which is as charming as a gorgeous lady. As you had suet jade necklace when you woke up, jade must be part of your life in the years."

A rebellious school dropout left home for a girl of his dream. They began a dangerous journey across rivers and into a wasteland and desert. Their love for each other was growing. There was someone else in their story—the old man, who had a piece of charming jade in his work-worn hand. They might be father and daughter, who were there as jade cutters.

"Do you mean I spent the years cutting jade? With the girl and her father?"

"It should be a good guess from what you have told me."

"A guess? But much of it was in your imagination."

"You're right. You must have held a lot back, or they're too difficult for words. Close your eyes now, and think if the episodes from your life in that period contrast sharply with my description."

I closed my eyes.

No.

They coincided. Zhong Yi's story mirrored what I had experienced. Her story was not a false one. I have been reviewing from time to time what had happened, as if I am flicking through an album with old photos.

Those were fragments I picked up from my memory of the past. I was surprised at how well Zhong Yi was reconstructing what had happened. It required great intuition and imagination, or she knew well what had happened. Damn it! Her feminine charm, which resided in part in her wisdom and power, had become a barrier for my independent judgment. Well, it also originated from the danger I had to face. When I was reaching my orgasm in bed with her the previous night, I was wondering if the woman, who was moaning and groaning like a love starved animal, was about to kill me.

I opened my eyes to smile at her.

"Yes, they were the same."

What she would do was more than reconstructing the happy time, if she was the guy.

"Are you sure?"

"Well, I might have missed an essential part of the memory. Even the fragments are still moving in a cold, dark, far-away shadow. Intuitively, I have avoided them. I have to say that they perturb me."

I was very "cooperative," keeping our conversation going her way, which was also my way.

The expression on her face when seeing the suet jade did not betray her, nor did her conversation about "the girl as pure as jade." When she did the same when analyzing my "memories that perturb," then she must have not involved herself in it.

I couldn't help thinking about how I snaked my tongue all over her the previous night. I drank in her perfect naked body, but it was nothing familiar.

Perhaps, it was someone else. I might have missed her so

much that her physical appearance had been turned into a feeling that engraved in my heart. I felt as if I had been blinded, but I could smell and hear her, in a way that went beyond the sense of sight.

"This uneasiness may be related to the injuries you had when you woke up."

If she was really her she would manage to stir up my memories, especially my memories of what had happened to me just before I woke up.

"Perhaps," I said.

"Have you ever tried to bring your memories back in the past years?"

"What?"

"Your experience in those five years has been a total mystery, which has become well known as your fame grows. Many people claim they saw you in the period, but a majority of them are sensational accounts. It seemed you didn't see any of them, and you have been coldly indifferent about your lost memories. So it's said you've made it all up."

I smiled without saying a word. It was safe not to say anything before I knew what she was looking for.

"Just like you try to avoid those 'disturbing memories' while being made about those lovely ones, you have chosen not to meet those eyewitnesses, which means you are unable to face your past in the subconscious. Your past is more than wind with the smell of grass and the gorgeous girl."

I remained silent.

"If you panned for jade, this is a convincing explanation why the witnesses, who worked together with you for a long time, haven't shown up. Jade dealers panned and sold jade, and they didn't mingle much with other people. They worked long hours in the wild. As a teenager, you could not be allowed to go to town to sell jade, so the girl and her father probably were the only people you met in those five years. But where are they now? Why haven't they stood out for you?"

"Because they were dead," I answered silently.

"There were a number of possibilities. They might have been abroad, knowing nothing about what you're doing, but this can't be true for someone as well-known as you. Or you may have been enemies later and decided not to see each other. There was one more possibility—they may have been deeply sorry for what had been done to you and escaped and would never come to you again."

No, they had been dead, I thought.

Why didn't she speak?

I sat up straighter, staring at her.

She was not looking at me, but it seemed she was thinking hard.

"What are you waiting for?" I had to make it clear with her, "but possibly, they may have been dead and it was me who killed them."

"You might be right, but if you killed them you couldn't be the murderer on the stage; nor could you be the murderer behind the garage at Dunhuang."

"Why not?"

"Your suspicion of yourself as the murderer of the girl and her father was from the bodily injuries you suffered, which seemed to have received from a bitter fighting. In other words, that could be the only time you killed, if you did it. You must have been with them before, unless they were involved in both of the two murders."

"You're being reasonable, but I see a paradox. I started to suspect that I may have killed when I read those stories, but what I did was not those described in the stories if I was the killer."

"Well, the problem you have is you've troubled with the idea that you killed, so much so that you have based your analyses on this paranoia, rather than logic. For example, the most likely explanation for the absence of the girl and her father is they are dead, but it doesn't mean you killed them. But it seems the two are naturally linked."

My heart beat missed a beat.

To tell a lie successfully when it is the point of departure, you need construct a new logic. Confronted by an opponent like Zhong Yi, even I found it hard to be able to think of everything.

"It seems to me you need to find a middle ground. It's wrong to take a position in advance—to presume that you were a killer. All your analyses should be based on the materials you have in hand. Your accounts of your memories don't offer sufficient proof that you killed, but they show a terrible thing must have happened to them, which made you sad. It has been buried deep in the category of your fond memories, becoming the source of your overriding concerns."

She gained the initiative easily, for which I almost stood up to give her a big hand. She did it like this: denying I was a killer to set my mind at ease before telling me "a terrible thing must have happened to them," which was seemingly in favor of me but would connect me with a serious crime. How tactical the mover was! Following this logic, I would have to admit it when the word "killer" was to be used to refer to me. If I were who I was playing, I would have to accept in the subconscious whatever she would say. You see, she hated to believe you were the killer and spoke in favor of you again and again, but the evidence all seemed to point to one conclusion: you killed. There was clearly no possibility of escape.

"Well, do you have a few sketchy details from a deeper level of your memory to add to what I've said or you might try to see what the 'disturbing feelings' you said are, and concentrate on the unsettling experience you've ignored so far and magnify them. Tell me whatever you see or think of during this process." Her tone of voice was low but silky.

I made a pretense of closing my eyes for a while, as if I was walking deep into my own consciousness.

"No," I said, opening my eyes. "I can't do it—probably because an opposite element has kept me out of it. Perhaps you can help."

"Me? But how?"

"You've got a great sense of intuition, and you have a very good visual imagination. Tell me whatever direction you think possible—a word, an image, a story. Put logic aside, and see if my memories can be brought back."

It was my last ditch attempt.

My open approach gave Zhong Yi much scope for creativity If she was the guy, she would be led to give some details of what had happened. I would go rather slow, until I had enough of her innermost secrets, before I would unmask her to reveal her identity.

"Do you mean divergent thinking? Without considering the logic?"

"Why don't you just follow your natural instinct? You're a highly intelligent woman," I said.

With her head slightly bowed, Zhong Yi doodled on her book.

For a moment I thought she was a snake ready to attack.

Then she raised her head.

"What are your other stories, in addition to 'In Jiayuguan' and 'In Dunhuang'?"

"'In Hetian' and 'In Kashgar,' but I failed in opening them, without the valid passwords. Like the other two, they must be about unsolved cases that took place in the years between 1994 and 1999."

"The two places are on our way, too." Her eyes met mine. With a deadpan expression on her face, she was trying to read the expression on mine.

"This morning you took us to the cave with the handprint, and I thought about it for quite a long time. It wasn't the place in 'In Dunhuang,' but you stopped in the middle when you explained why you did it. You looked as if ..." She paused as if she was wondering what to say next, but the silence lengthened.

I was silent, too, with no intention of picking up the threads of the conversation.

As our itinerary coincided exactly with the one described in the story, some change had been expected in our journey. The person who was trying to trap me would have no other choice but keep me as a companion, if he or she did not want to lose control of the situation. To identify who the person was, I took them to the caves, because no other people knew it was not the place in "In Dunhuang." I had expected a change of expression on his or her face, but I failed. There was something queer about every one of them. Chen Ailing smoked less than she had done on the opera stage and in the garage. Fan Sicong overacted almost exaggeratedly. Zhong Yi seemed remarkably calm or absent-minded. Yuan Ye refused to go with us. As all of them were suspicious-looking, I was left hugely disappointed.

As Zhong Yi reverted to the subject now, she must have sensed I was testing the water. But she was hesitating, because she was among the suspects.

Why did she come to the topic?

"To tell you the truth, I find it rather strange," she continued.

"That was a great move. Well, I don't think you would disagree," she said, glancing at me. I knew it would be great if I could make up a convenient excuse to disagree when I realized it was too late after my subconscious silence.

It was a great guess, but what harm were there when I frankly admitted it?

She continued, "This is what you are. I mean the book is the man and from your books I can tell you're a man who plans everything down to the last detail but holds initiative as well. It was this man who had managed to identify the suspect, but changed his idea after he passed the garage. And he had to come to me for a psychiatric treatment. I can't say you were telling lies, but what you told me is rather weird. You were being different from who you are in my eyes, and you were not being who you have been as a writer. I didn't expect you're so weak; you should have pretended otherwise even if you're weak and rather suspect you were the murderer. Yes, you went to bed with me, but so what?"

"You're different," I said.

She smiled, sticking out her tongue at me with a look of amusement in her eyes.

"It's an old argument, but I think there's truth in it. It's rather late tonight and I'm sleepy and my imagination would go wild. How about tomorrow? If you do the same tomorrow, I would tell you whatever I have in my mind. You're not a guy who would continue to pretend otherwise when your lie is exposed."

I walked her to the door and waved her goodbye.

"Did you have your gloves on when you woke up with all those injuries?"

I was surprised.

"I have avoided such questions, but from a psychological point of view, this partiality of yours—whether because of your fetish about cleanliness or not—is a vital part of your mental state. So, I'll answer your question tomorrow if you insist."

It was not her.

I closed the door. Easing myself into the armchair, I saw her pen left on the tea table.

Or was she a tough opponent?

I tried to figure out if she was a good enough calculating, resourceful actress?

She was naive and honest, as I knew her.

But anyone who survived what she had experienced would be a different person. It was the distillation of life.

She asked me one last question before she closed the door: if I was the guy who designed all this by way of my stories, when would the crucial moment come?

Her question was asked as a challenge to the apparent sincerity I had been trying to show tonight.

But it was phrased so casually that I sensed an air of intimacy on her face.

"It's something I have to think about," I answered and then

gave her a peck on the check before I left.

It was a question framed for my standpoint, which would be clear to her however I answered it.

But it was a good one. Where and when would they kill me, if they had planned to do it?

In Jiayuguan, Dunhuang, Hetian, or Kashgar? They would naturally choose Kashgar, our destination, but on a second thought they would do it unexpectedly in Hetian.

It would have most probably happened in Kashgar!

The murder on the stage was committed as revenge and that in the garage to experience the sensual pleasure of brutal killing. The one described in "In Hetian" was still to know because I failed in opening it, but did it have something to do with a cold-blooded murder after rape? All the energy for death was gathering for an explosion in Kashgar, wasn't it? As the place was where all had started, it should have been where they ended. What happened in Jiayuguan and Dunhuang were too ceremonial, for death or revenge. When such a dramatic announcement was chosen, it would be unusual to end it earlier in Hetian simply to surprise.

It could only have happened in Kashgar, nowhere else.

Sitting in the armchair facing the entrance to my room, I fixed my eyes on the door, wondering how the murderer would approach me. It seemed that there was a subtle change of light.

I tried to concentrate, but the door was what it had been.

Trying to remember what I had seen, I came to realize that it was something lighting up, but it was such a slight change that I even doubted if it had ever happened.

Then I thought about it in a different way—what on the door could cause such a slight change before me?

When my eyes travelled over the door, it all clicked.

Peephole.

Light from the corridor may have come in only when she walked away from the peephole. As the corridor was carpeted, she was not making any noise. Without the light from the peephole, I would have never known Zhong Yi had been outside.

What was she doing outside?

I rushed over to pull the door open. She wouldn't have the time to return to her room.

It was Zhong Yi, but she was not walking away. She was coming to my room, smiling at me.

"I forgot to take my pen with me."

I turned for it and handed it over to her. With a "Thanks and good night," she went back.

I watched her walking to her door, swiping her door card, going in the room and closing the door behind her, but she didn't turn her face back.

It was a terribly pale face.

Chapter VI To Disturb

Today's journey, from Korla through Luntai to Taklimakan Desert, was more than seven hundred kilometers. We would spend the night in a small town in the desert.

The plan of itinerary had included half of day's tour to the Flaming Mountain and we would spend the night at Korla. But I chose not to visit it, so that I could have more time in Hetian and Kashgar. Exhausted business travelers in old times must be in no mood for sightseeing in the vast desert and their only wish would be to reach their destinations as early as possible. Following their footsteps, I would rather choose to feel what they felt about the journal.

Of course, I was trying to be reasonable by saying so, but my true purpose was not to waste my time on the way. I visited Hetian and Kashgar simply out of consideration for others.

I had to be considerate for those who were trying to set a trap for me. The best place for trap would be nowhere but in Hetian or Kashgar. So I needed to allow them the time to prepare for it, didn't I?

As the trap was there, I would choose to go for it. But I would do it so to free myself from it.

I was fully confident of beating them.

I knew well that confidence was different from arrogance. Although I had become the target, I knew I could manage to protect myself for a couple of times, but I could never live in a constant fear. This was why I decided to go for it, once for all. As my enemy was fully prepared, I had to be ready to fight. If I handled it clumsily, it would cost my life. My strategy was to go for it and disturb.

To disturb is to change, to add unexpected uncertainty to the situation. Put simply, I was about to be a trouble to them. I had no idea which of my companions would be the trap-setter (or trap-setters, when I would explore all possibilities), so I had to deal with each of them.

For Zhong Yi, I used the way that all men preferred. Bodily fluids didn't help, but they brought up many questions. I was doomed to death if I was not able to decide on bed whether she was the one who laid the trap. As I believed she was the most likely suspect, I talked with her every night as a psychotherapist as well.

My strategy for Fan Sicong was also effective for Zhong Yi, because I was having an affair with her, the woman of his heart. He must have been left raging at me, gnashing his teeth. If he was the trap-setter, I was sure I could make him show his true self.

The starting point in dealing with Yuan Ye was his girlfriend, who I wouldn't care more, otherwise. But now he talked about her to me whenever he was free, for my analyses of the text messages they exchanged and my suggestions as to what to do next. The great passion he felt for her and the role I played in their relation would lead him to an easy mistake, especially at the crucial moment, if he was my enemy (which was least possible among the four).

As for Chen Ailing, I didn't have any idea yet. But I knew my success in dealing with her depended on how I would deal with the thing that mattered most to her. What I did must be able to affect her emotionally, which would, in turn, disrupt her rhythm. In other words, I had to know what her weak point was. This is interesting, isn't it? The thing that matters most to someone is where his weak point lies.

To find Chen Ailing's weak point, I had to start from her habit of smoking. I saw her smoking only twice in the past days—on the stage and in the garage, when I told stories of murder scenes. She took long puffs at her cigarettes, seeming to be enjoying it immensely. I could see she had been deeply affected and, as a result, she had to smoke to keep herself calm. It usually meant earlier emotional wounds or personal secrets, or both. I would know the perfect way to disturb her, if I could learn about them. She loved reading my stories and watching American crime series, a hobby which probably shared the same reason with her habit of smoking at scenes of crimes. Talking about her love of American series, I had asked rather causally whether her husband and children had the same hobby, but she evaded it. This was an unusual reaction. It told me more than she loved crime stories: probably, she had a family that was not a traditional type. All these details must be interlocked and form a circle.

But, as I remembered, I didn't see her smoking when I told the made-up story at the grottoes. If her desire for cigarettes when I described the details of a crime was one of her behavioral patterns, her reaction at the grottoes could be interpreted in different ways: either because my story ended too soon and her emotion was still to build up to the level that a cigarette was needed or because she knew I was talking nonsense and the place for the story in "In Dunhuang" was a garage at the edge of the desert while nothing happened at the grottoes.

So, Chen Ailing would be the second potential suspect, only next to Zhong Yi. I had to do something to her as early as possible, before it was too late.

But a bumping vehicle in the day's journey was not a place for an effective communication with her. To encourage her to let me into her secrets, a pleasant environment was needed, where I could try a variety of tricks. It was impossible in a car with several others, no matter how hard I would try.

What I could do was to chat with her in a rather informal manner. I asked her what American series she liked most; which episodes of *CSI* or *Criminal Minds* were best and which were like trash. I had had no time to focus my attention on her and didn't talk much with her, and I was trying to make it up.

In addition, I started flirting with Zhong Yi when I got in the vehicle this morning, which gave the impression that we were together last night. She was visibly unhappy about it, which was what I wanted because Fan Sicong looked even more uneasy. Then he fumbled all the way for something to talk about with her. How tolerant he was of her even when he knew what was happening between the woman and me. He didn't care about being a third wheel.

When the driver stopped his vehicle for us to smoke and use the toilets, Yuan Ye would be busy texting. Of course he needed my help. He tried his best to persuade his girlfriend that his wrong message was for a friend, but she was guessing who the friend was by excluding all his female friends one by one. I discouraged him, "Things will only get worse if you continue like this. Tell her 'Stop it now,' and let her be. Ignore it whatever she would say; don't take her calls. Do what I say and then send her a long heartfelt text message at night—it would be the knockout blow."

Asked how to write the message, I told him the main points and style were the key. "After some shared memories to start, hint darkly you already know she cheated you. Make sure you don't overdo it, to spare her blushes. At the same, you have to let her know you still have a lot of feeling for her. Then you come to your memories together again before you end with sweet nothings and promises. You do it in four paragraphs. Don't mention the other woman she imagined. Nor do you have to answer any of the questions she asked when she was mad."

We had lunch in Korla, but when we were about to leave, we discovered we had got a flat left front tire. It was not a slow puncture, so it won't help to pump it up. As the desert area was ahead, we had to have it fixed, rather than use the spare tire. I was rather sleepy after lunch and collapsed onto a sofa in the garage. As we had to wait for a new tire from a different place, I drifted into a nap.

I awoke to hear Fan Sicong and Zhong Yi talking about Luobu Village, which I had crossed off from the itinerary. Hearing Fan Sicong say it was a pity not to go there, I found it the right time to make fun of him, telling them the village in Weili was actually a new man-made spot for tourists. "The Taklimakan desert expanded greatly in the years from 1950 to 1970, reducing the forest of poplars to half of its size and driving the local residents away. How come there are Luobu people left for you?"

Fan Sicong got embarrassed and upset, which cheered me up.

Zhong Yi came to his rescue by asking where their descendents were now. I told her they intermarried with Uighurpeople. There was a clan of Luobu near Korla, perhaps the largest group in the whole area, but their traditions were no longer followed faithfully, as half of them were descendants of mixed parentage.

Zhong Yi said it was a pity that the minority group would disappear on the Earth in about several decades. I responded by saying such things were unavoidable and they were part of our life. In the last hundred year numerous minorities had been assimilated into Han; many of those officially recognized ones were ethical groups only in name and they were basically Han at heart. Those distinctively different ones often disagreed with Han and created continuing ethical conflicts in the country, which, in turn, helped them keep their heritages alive. Uyghur, which assimilated Luobu, was among them.

Fan Sicong suggested that we visit the village as it was quite close, saying there would be nothing to see when they disappeared in the near future.

I found it funny that he pretended how well-educated he was on the ground of non-material heritage protection. "There's nothing to see now. A Uighurvillage, with no houses on trees," I said. But when I thought it would be a nice chance for me to talk with Chen Ailing, I changed my mind. "Why not? It's on our way."

The car had been ready for some time, but they didn't wake me up, as I was soundly asleep. The village was somewhere between Heshilike Township and Tuobuliqi Township, and some of the residents lived on jade dealings. As I had been there more than a decade ago, it must have changed beyond my reorganization.

I did not remember exactly what the village name was, but knew its general location. I asked a Uighur woman with a mole at the corner of her eyebrow about "the place where Luobu people live." The car stuttered along a dirt road to the opposite side of a hill. When I came across a tree growing sideways out of a stream, I came to realize we were approaching a field outside the village. The slope nearby was covered with small *mazha*, "graves" in the local language, which had gray round tops looking like mushrooms. In the graves lay generations of the deceased.

As it was not a tourist destination and the local people were also known as somewhat clubby, a vehicle with strangers would be considered aggressive. The car was parked by the side of the road and Yuan Ye stayed to take care of it.

I flashed a smile at Yuan Ye. "You've got to wait and don't spoil your entire effort. Remember you answered the message at the garage."

"Sure, I will. I will do what you said and wait until it's dark."

Fan Sicong and Zhong Yi lagged behind. "Soon you'll see *mazha*, an overhead projection over a street, a mosque and *naan* bread stove, so it's just like any other Uighur village," I told Fan Sicong with a smile, when we were at the entrance of the village.

"It doesn't matter at all. I'll see what a Uighur village looks like, and I like exotic styles."

"Really? I know what you're interested in," I joked with him.

His face flushed with embarrassment. It must be because I had been in bed with the woman of his heart.

The village was halfway up a hill. A dirt lane ran all the way down from the entrance. It would be churned into mud in a rainy day, but obviously it seldom rained here. The stream was nowhere to see—it must have its course.

On one side of the road were mostly two-storied buildings. They were all with adobe walls and next to each other. The rich and the poor families could be recognized immediately as we passed—some had a yard with figs, some had an open corridor, but others had simply an ordinary wooden gate. On the other side was not a high cliff—it was only a few meters deep. It was the stream and I heard the bubbling sound.

The village was on an uneven terrain. The main road formed a U shape, and it branched off at several places, leading to different rows of houses.

A typical Uighur village, it looked it had been there for generations of residents for at least a hundred years. As I had visited different places in the northwestern province, I felt nothing unusual about it. But Zhong Yi, Fan Sicong, and the others were all excited about the special, exotic style, which was different from buildings in other parts of China. They were just like northerners who were visiting a small southern town for the first time. Fan Sicong was busy taking pictures, lagging way behind us. For a while, I wondered how he could be enjoying himself so much while he was expected to shoot me for the trip. On second thoughts, I was happy that I was left alone with Chen Ailing.

It was rather quiet in the village. We did not see a single

young man or woman after we were there for quite a while. Most of the gates were open, but the yards were all free of people. I spotted an old man sitting in one of them—he was with a small hat and looked at us in silence when we passed. The other people around us were two kids who were enjoying their paddle in an open area by a stream.

We had no idea how much traditional culture the villagers had retained. We had hardly enough time to scratch the surface.

Walking slowly on the dirt lane, I was beginning to feel a bit chilly, in a time when local people were in short sleeves. What I felt was only psychological, because this village looked more like a ghost town. Of course, it was not a deserted village—there must be more women inside the adobe houses busy with their needlework, in addition to the old man and the kids. But I had a feeling of coldness and emptiness. It was unusual for a crime writer with a twisted mind who got vicarious thrills from visiting scenes of crimes. The change must have to do with the discomfort I was suffering.

When did the discomfort start? It seemed I began to feel it when the old man with a hat on his head stared at me.

It was like a sound, an invisible and voiceless sound, which came from the open yard, the eyes of the old man, and the cracks on the wall and drifted along all the way to wrap me up. It was a low humming sound, a hustling sound, and a chirruping sound, which came in from my left ear and out from my right one, but remained in my body. It was a familiar sound, but it was actually non-existent.

I did not like the village, and I regretted I was here.

I attempted to confine my attention to Chen Ailing.

We talked about crimes and killings.

When we came to American TV series, I found her interest growing. She became wildly excited and her eyes rounded when talking about the scene of a crime, a post mortem examination or the motive for a murder. I discovered her pupils dilated, which could never be phony reaction, but a natural physical response.

Thinking about the times she chose to smoke, I was sure the crucial breakthrough was coming.

I did not think she had been born to kill. She must have been traumatized with something, which would help me in my success to disturb her.

"Actually, profiling has its own limitations and can be unreliable, in the same way that fleeting expressions are often exaggerated by actors or actresses. Mental processes are beyond the ability of any psychologist. All they can do is to give us sketches, sometimes misleading ones."

"How about you? It seems your analyses of the head on the city wall and the cause for the daughter's death came from your profiling work. So ..."

"I was not doing profiling analyses," I interrupted her. "I depended more on my nose."

I pointed my nose with my finger. "I've got a good nose for murderous lunatics, which relies on my intuition rather than formulaic profiling."

"You think your intuition is more reliable?"

"When it works, it is as if you feel a sudden flash of understanding, or you're inside the body of someone, who is possessed by you. It's something you're born with. If you believe a murderer leaves his psychological frequency behind at the crime scene, I can detect the signal intuitively. From my point of view, a flash of intuition takes both apparent and unapparent details and clues into consideration and makes a conclusion in a minute, which is a more advanced form of intellectual activity."

Chen Ailing was trying to understand what I had meant, with a puzzled frown in her eyes. My nonsense words, but equivocal, was misleading to anyone.

My face creased into a frown, too, as I started to grow uneasy again.

"Did you hear any noise?" I couldn't help asking her.

"You mean just now? No, I didn't. What was it?"

"Oh, nothing." I shook my head.

My phone vibrated in my pocket. I took it out and looked at it, and my eyes narrowed.

It was an MMS from an unfamiliar number. In addition to a voice message, I could see only a few words: "It's the time."

I clicked on the audio butter and put the phone to my ear. I didn't know what it was yet, but I was care enough so that Chen Ailing wouldn't overhear it.

Nothing but laughter.

Voice of a woman.

It was two or three seconds long. It was somewhat clear, somewhat sharp, somewhat unsteady, but with a strange tone.

Nothing else except the laughter.

I played it a second time, and then a third time, listening hard. There was no background noise. As I listened to it more, it became somewhat familiar to me.

It's all an illusion, I thought. The illusion was created simply because I was trying to match it with what I had in mind. I was misled psychologically by my own way of thinking. "The two people are distinctively different, and their voices are distinctively different. It's impossible!"

Chen Ailing stared at me. I was sure she had got the feeling that something was going wrong, but she chose not to ask.

I put my phone back into my pocket, but I was growing uneasy inside.

"It's the time, it's the time," I kept repeating the message quietly over and over again. And then I realized Chen Ailing was with me. As anyone reacts instinctively at similar moments, I tried to disguise by continue the conversation with her, but the topic escaped me, leaving me embarrassed with my mouth open.

I placed my right hand on my face, and began to dig my thumb fingernail deep into the flesh of my temple. I smiled apologetically before I stepped aside, took out my phone and called back.

I would not escape, as I always did. I would face it, no matter what I would have to deal with.

I was fully prepared for a fight. But it turned out that I boxed at shadows.

The telephone number was no longer in service!

It didn't exist.

But the laughter was from it a moment ago.

"Must be some malicious software. It only disguised itself as a telephone number," I guessed.

Putting my phone back into my pocket, I started to walk up leisurely, as if nothing had happened, pretending that I wanted to see what the village was like, as my interest in the topic had waned. Anyway, I was a person who acted on impulse, or an unpredictable man, they may say. Chen Ailing was not surprised, because she had got to know me more as a companion. She walked behind me, looking around.

While, she was staring, my eyes followed hers to my hands. I was folding my arms on my chest, a subconscious posture that I was not aware of. It was a typical body language of rejection, a sign of defense due to an inside sense of danger.

The old woman had sharp eyes.

It would be make-believe if I had a change in posture, but I felt painfully awkward to continue walking with my arms folded, as I had been fully aware of my problem.

It was all because of the pressure under which I was put, the pressure from the message. The village added to the pressure as well, which was building up as I approached it, fleeing the nagging lump of tension in my chest.

It was coming? They were about to take action? I had thought it was highly likely that they would strike the first blow in Kashgar or Hetian. Why this place?

Who else knew I was here?

There was movement behind me. I turned and saw Zhong Yi and Fan Sicong.

They lagged way behind, didn't they? I remembered they had taken a different path at the fork. I had no idea when they had caught up.

Well, my attention had been taken away. And I found it was still wandering. I had been held in an invisible camp made of my niggling worries, the intense pressure, and the impending danger coming to me.

It was decidedly risky.

And, it was decidedly unusual. How did I become such a different man? It was too bad to feel that I had lost control of myself.

"Ha ha!" A voice coming from behind me said in my ear.

I turned my head immediately.

Who was there? It was neither Zhong Yi nor Fan Sicong. They were discussing about an iron sign above the gate of a house, on which were ten stars, with words "law, morals, service, patriot," and others, in both Mandarin and Uygur. Yes, yes, they had been talking about the sign in the previous minute. Zhong Yi was in the middle of her sentence when the laughter was heard. "It's just like the sign of 'Family of the Year'," she said. She finished her sentence, so she didn't laugh. Nor did Fan Sicong. There was nothing that would make him laugh at the moment. And it was a woman's voice.

The voice was somewhat clear, somewhat sharp, and somewhat unsteady.

Yes, it was the voice in the message.

"Yes, I see. But what's the star for technology? Is the farmer an inventor?" Fan Sicong asked.

"Maybe he's a student of technology, or he uses some technology in his farm," Zhong Yi thought for a few seconds before she answered.

They didn't hear the laughter!?

It was so clear that it was ringing in my ears. But none of the three of them hear anything?

Was I hearing things?

I didn't know if there were ghosts, but I had never included them in my stories. I did write about people who appeared as ghosts, but they were people.

It was unlikely now that the three of them had ganged up and been willfully deaf to the noise. Or was it from a sounder for certain direction and some people could not hear the noise?

It could also be all an illusion—I had been too stressed and heard a sound that did not exist, which I denied immediately because I knew I had been right. My whole life had been based on the belief that I had been right.

There was a throbbing in my temples. My head began to hurt me when I thought more about it.

Then another noise was heard.

It was a noise beyond my description, as if it was from someone who signed when he or she was caught by the throat or from a rusted door that was pulled open with force—a horrible sharp one.

Was it produced by a human? After a moment of panic, I glanced around and was delighted to know they all heard it from the change of expressions on their faces.

"What was that awful noise?" Fan Sicong asked.

"Seemed it was from that direction," Zhong Yi answered, pointing to a branch road in front of us.

"Shall we go and have a look?" Fan Sicong walked as fast as he could to pass me and turned to the road.

I followed him. It was a sharp noise and I guessed the source was about a hundred steps away.

We turned the corner and saw a plump Uighur woman standing before her own gate with her back toward us. Hearing the noise, she turned around. She looked rather uneasy.

She was out to see what was happening too. When I was about to ask her about it, she went into the gate and slammed the door shut behind her.

A few steps forward, we saw on our side a cave, in which stood a black goat, which stared at us. The atmosphere was immediately charged with mysteriousness. We were wondering if the noise came from the cave when we were called by someone from behind. It was the Uighur woman, who leaned precariously out of the door. With her Mandarin Chinese with heavy local accent, she shouted after us, but only I understood what she meant.

"She told us not to go forward," I told my companions.

As she was willing to talk with us, we turned to asked her what was happening.

"Don't go there," she said. "It's a dangerous place."

I asked what the place was, why it was dangerous, and where the noise came from. But it seemed she refused to tell us strangers more about it. The only thing she told us was a house was left empty and the owners were all dead.

When I switched to Uighur, she told us most of the story. There had lived a couple with their son and daughter. The two men, who had been in the trade of jade, were killed one day when they were out of town. In the sparsely populated Xinjiang Uyghur Autonomous Region, where people by nature were tough, things did happen unexpectedly. I had heard a lot of stories about how human lives were cheaper than jade. People had not been shocked when they were told someone was murdered. What had shocked them was that one day the mother disappeared, leaving alone the girl of seven or eight years old, who had been taken care of by her neighbors. But soon the girl disappeared, too, leaving the house empty.

When the mother had not been seen, rumor had it that she had left with a man, leaving her little girl alone. When the daughter disappeared, it was said the mother loved her daughter so much that she came to take her away, which was a fair assumption. As nobody had witnessed when and how they left the village, baseless rumors about ghosts began to spread as time passed on. At the beginning, a few villagers had managed to appropriate the house, but they had to give the idea up, leaving it to gather dust. It had been said the girl was seen one day many years later when the gate was left open in the wind; weird sounds were also heard on rainy or windy nights. Some even believed that the girl had never left the house. A *mazha*, a cenotaph, had been built last year for the family and it seemed fewer strange things had happened. But the sound was heard again today.

The Uighur woman must have thought we would be frightened away by her stories, but I asked her which house it was. Staring at me disbelievingly for a second, she told me it was the house with a drawing on its wall before she closed her gate hurriedly.

The two of us talked for a while in Uighur, which my colleagues were not able to understand. They asked me to explain what we were talking about, but I was not in the mood and walked along in the front.

Walking about two dozens of steps farther, I passed gates with traditional Chinese antithetical couplets on the two sides and decorative carvings on bricks, but none of them had a drawing or even a New Year painting on them. It looked somewhat a deserted section when we turned a corner, with only a couple of houses before us, beyond which were some *mazha* among trees and rocks. On the rising ground in the distance were some small round graves, and halfway up a steep hill was a bigger one inside a yard with adobe walls. The latter one had been built for respected members in the village and used to be called a *mazha*, which was now an umbrella term for all graves. The one for the four dead from the family must be among the smaller ones, but I had no idea which one it wasAs no drawing was seen on any gate before me, I started to wonder if I had misunderstood the woman.

A few steps farther, I saw it. It was not a drawing taped on the gate as I had expected, but a fresco, which was rare in the region and, perhaps the only one in the village. Between the gate and a window was a well-structured hollow in the shape of house—a terraced roof and a square-shaped body. The fresco was in the square. The colors had faded over the years. It looked rather pale in a distance, but as I approached it I was able to recognize what it portrayed.

It was not something unusual. A blue vase was in the middle and flourishing plants grew out of its mouth. Above the vase was a patch of darkening blue—probably the sky—and under it was some decorative lines that looked like vines. The two sections in the lower corners were not exactly the same, but they were identical and I thought they were so because there was a dry leaf covering part of the lower right corner.

"Here?" Fan Sicong asked.

I didn't answer her, my eyes fixed on the leaf.

It was the only leaf on the wall, an incongruous sight on the picture before our eyes. I was wondering how a leaf could stick on a dry wall.

I took it down. And I saw a brown spot on the picture, and the leaf ...

"Blood. Is it blood?" Fan Sicong cried out.

I placed the leaf before my nose to smell it.

"It is, and it isn't completely dry," I said.

"Human blood?" he asked even before I could finish my sentence.

I was wondering how anyone could tell if it was human blood by smelling it. My emotions were churning, as if my head was boiling with competing ideas. Not at all in mood for a conversation, I simply answered, "Yes, it is."

Zhong Yi gulped.

This woman is no different from Fan Sicong, I thought, but in no time I realized that she was shocked at the drawing, rather than the blood. Under the leaf were a few bold brush strokes which formed a horizontal human face.

It was a weird face of a child.

It looked like a small head on a body of vines. With the sky on the top and the land at the bottom, it seemed the boy was buried in the earth. While his body had already mixed with the soil, where the vines grew, the head was still out there.

"Here we are," I said. "The noise we heard must be from this house."

After a pause, I continued, "This is an empty house, and the owners were all dead."

"You want to go in?" Zhong Yi asked.

The gate, which was made of two pieces of planks, was to the left of the fresco. It was closed, but not latched. I pushed it open easily.

I walked away from the sunlight into the room, taking a deep breath which, I imagined, contained all the secrets to what had happened in the room. It was my way to tell whoever was waiting for me that I was coming.

It was the time for me to come.

And it felt great.

Yes, it was great. The discomfort that had been troubling me was lessening as I entered. The room was filled with a smell beyond my description. It was neither the smell of a flower nor the stench of a rotten body, but it wafted around me, as if a heart was beating noisily in the depth of the darkness or a lock of black hair was brushing against the back of my neck. It felt better, because I had been restless when I was in the sunlight. I felt I was shivering slightly, as if I was given a mild electric shock, which kept me more clear-headed and focused.

Yes, more focused, because there was something here waiting for me and seducing me.

Was it my fate?

It was a small square-shaped room. Under my feet were squared-shaped tiles, and over my head were four-layered block-shaped Uighur decorative patterns. These buildings were adobe ones, but they were beautifully decorated inside. The decorations had four layers of colors—purple, yellow, light blue, and orange, but they had faded. Light came in from the window of two meters in height and a circular column of light was formed in the room, in which particles of dust were dancing. It was extremely dry here, but it felt strangely damp and chilly.

It was the living room, with two round stools and two long wooden benches around a square table and a large wardrobe against a wall. The furniture was left as it had been, which indicated that the villagers were rather superstitious.

There were doors in front and on both sides. They were all elegantly designed two-leaved doors, with carved patterns on the top. They were glass-paneled, or rather, they had been glass-paneled, as only a few glass splinters were left on them.

I walked around and the small splinters of broken glass screeched under my feet.

Had the glass been broken just before I arrived? I did not see any dust on the jagged glass on the door. I dropped my head, staring at the jumble of fragments of glass and the dust on the ground. If it was broken a moment ago, did it have to do with the noise? And the pattern formed by the jumble looked like …

It seemed that my mind had been controlled by a mysterious force, but Zhong Yi started to talk.

"I feel quite … uncomfortable in here," she said.

I was about to get somewhere, but my train of thought was interrupted.

Chen Ailing was not following us. She walked very slowly, probably hesitating over whether to come in. Fan Sicong imparted to Zhong Yi for a few words of wisdom, and they went into the door on the left.

I chose the one on the right.

It was as simple in structure as the living-room. There was not a single person in it, and I could see no hiding place. It was a bedroom, with the bed against the wall. The coverlet was red, with a red and yellow blanket on it. A purple quilt was left carelessly on a corner of the bed. It seemed the owner left in a hurry.

The high window was behind a curtain, so the room was rather dark. I was about to step out when I set my eyes on the part of the coverlet that covered the bed frame. I started to wonder whether the base was a solid one, although the bed of its kind was usually so structured.

I crouched down and slowly took up one of its corners.

My mind clamped down as I did it, as if something evil under it would jump out at me.

Of course, nothing happened. As I expected, before me was a four-layer brick base and a mattress on it.

I shook my head and was about to stand up when I felt a nasty blow on the head.

Ouch!

I didn't know what to do.

I had made sure there were no hiding places in the room, and I was alert enough to check the bed. I was also all ears, but I had heard nothing but my footsteps. Had someone approached me without a sound? It was impossible for anyone to do it on a floor covered with broken glass, unless he or she was barefooted.

Or it was simply not human?

I asked myself the question several times—within seconds. The strike left me on the floor, my back leaning against the bed and my hands supporting me on the floor. I looked up, but not a single soul was before me.

I put my hand on my forehead, finding it was hard for me to breathe. Maybe I had missed a place? Trying to avoid a second strike, I rolled on the ground, but so clumsily that I lost my balance and struck my shoulder firmly on something solid.

Wait.

It was a sewing machine. It was near the bed. I suddenly realized that it was also the sewing machine that hurt me on the forehead—I hurt myself on the sharp corner of the board when I stood up.

Pushing myself to my feet with my hand on the bed, I squinted to examine the machine.

It hurt me twice, but it was not crucial.

Why hadn't I seen it?

I had thought I had had the full view of the room when I entered, but I had missed the machine beside the bed. I hit my head on its board when I rose to my feet after my checking of the bed frame. It meant that I was beside the machine. But I had not at all noticed it and had thought I had been attacked long after I was hurt.

I hurt myself on it, but how could I make such a mistake? This means ...

I patted the old machine gently and went out of the room.

No one was in the living room. Chen Ailing must remain outside, and Fan Sicong and Zhong Yi, who entered the other room, were nowhere to be seen. I even couldn't hear any sound of their footsteps. Everything was quiet, as if the whole world had changed after I entered the room.

I got a sneaky feeling that I had been left alone.

My forehead kept hurting me.

The driving force behind me emerged again. I knew it was an illusion, but I followed it and walked to the front door.

I pushed open the unlocked door, and right in front of me was a big, scarlet armchair. It was not a place for it, as if a translucent person in it was staring at me. The chair was almost free of dust, and it seemed it was used daily. Of course, I knew it was because of the wind. Behind the back of the chair was the back door, which was open and wind was coming from the backyard.

It was another hall, a dining room perhaps. Instead of examining the room and the obtrusive chair, I weaved around it quickly and entered the backyard through a door.

I did so because I heard some noise.

In a similar scene in mystery stories it is usually a low moan of despair, a weeping sound, a sad melody, or a faint stirring.

But what I heard was laughter.

It was a fit of laughter from a woman. It was a giggle. Was it from a girl?

It stopped when I entered the yard, as if a woman, somewhere in the deserted house, was play at hide-and-seek with me.

I looked around, trying to figure out who it was, before I moved two steps to the right and leant up against a wall. The yard was about two hundred square meters, with a hill on one side and mud walls on the right and left sides. Dry vines twined around grape trellises.

The laughter was heard again. It was so faint that I was scared, but I was sure it was ahead of me on the right.

I walked up until I was close to the wall, removed a clump of bushes, and saw a deep hole under it.

The laughter must have come from the hole.

Whoever did it was vicious. To enter the hole would be dangerous, but should I leave silently? Or should I be as timid as a little girl and go for others so we could go into it together?

The noise was heard, so I would have no other choice. "This is what life is—there are roads all around you, but you can only choose one direction."

The hole led to a cellar, with very narrow stairs. I had to stoop down. The light fell in a pool at the bottom, which was about seven to eight meters from the opening, but beyond it was all dark.

It was about ten degrees centigrade or even lower in the cool and dark cellar. There was a carpet of straw on the ground, which rustled under my feet. This place had a dry climate and it seldom rained. A similar cellar in the open in the South would be like a small pool.

The cellar was not empty. Before me were four shelves independent of each other, and the other ends of them were in the dark. They should not be too long—no more than ten meters, as I could see about five meters of them with the dim light.

The shelves were full of baskets, which, I could tell from their arrangements, were for grapes. The last batch of the fruits was put in the cellar for use in the coming spring. The opening of cellar was usually covered. It was open now, probably because the cover had been removed when searching for a missing person, but had not moved back.

I did not step softly on purpose when I entered, so that my footsteps sounded on the stairs. When I stepped into a place with dim light and paused, I heard my own breathing, which sounded much louder in the quiet cellar. As I breathed in and out, it seemed the air between the shelves was disturbed.

As I was adapting to the darkness, I moved forward slowly. I was not going to use my telephone to light my way. The crucial moment was coming, and I needed my hands free to deal with whatever to come.

Among the three passages between the four shelves, I chose the one on the rightmost. I did it for the same reason that I had chosen to stand near a wall when I entered the backyard. When one was exposed to a potential danger, it was wise to be near a wall, because it was least possible that the danger came from inside the wall.

"One, two, three, four, five, six, seven," I counted by steps.

Slowly and cautiously, I moved forward, the hairs on my arms prickling with fear.

"Eight, nine, ten, eleven, twelve, thirteen, fourteen, fifteen."

I reached the end.

My steps were smaller than usual, so the cellar was about seven to eight meters deep. The shelves on my sides were full of baskets, without any exception.

I had the desire to see what was in the baskets with the help of my phone, but I suppressed it.

There was a gap between the shelves and the wall. I made a left turn without any pause, but I turned my head and saw the dim outlines leading to the light at the entrance, with no other objects in my sight. It was always a better view when observing things in a brighter place.

I returned from the passage on my left.

"One, two, three, four, five, six, seven, eight, nine, ten, eleven, twelve, thirteen, fourteen, and fifteen."

Step by step, I went back to the pool of light, free from any danger and without hearing any noise other than my footsteps on the floor. The source of laughter was somewhere in the cellar, but it was not heard again.

No sense of relief swept over me—I could feel the unresolved tension.

I'm here, but you're still in the dark. When will you come out? I thought.

I thought I had been cooperative enough, and now I would go back. But I did not think I would be allowed to leave so easily, because I had been enticed to come, whoever it was.

I was frozen when I raised my head before I was about to go up the stairs.

I saw someone in front of me.

To be exact, I saw two feet, oh no, a pair of shoes.

Shoes for children.

They were small red leather ones. I looked up and saw a white skirt but nothing else. It appeared to me that a girl was sitting at the mouth of the hole.

The feet remained still, so no noise was made. But they started to swing slightly as I caught sight of them, making a clicking sound again the edge of the opening.

Click, click, click, click.

The sound echoed faintly through the empty cellar.

The laughter was then heard again.

It was from behind me.

I made an abrupt turn.

It stopped, but a long female sign followed.

It was from my left side, the passage ahead of me on the left, through which I had passed.

All of a sudden, darkness gathered around me, and I could see the pool of light ahead fading and in no time I was in pitch darkness. I turned my head and I caught the last glimpse of light from the opening. The cellar was left in inky darkness.

The entrance was covered!

Unable to see anything, I stood still.

Instead of reaching out for my telephone, I raised my hand to feel my forehead. It had been hurting me ever since I struck my head on the sewing machine. I must be bleeding.

Then I began to laugh.

I laughed, but silently. I knew I should keep silent, so I managed to stifle my laughter. I doubled up with it, with one hand over my mouth and the other pressing my stomach. I didn't think even a weird voice from the depth of the darkness could stop me.

It lasted as long as half a minute. Yes, I thought I laughed for such a long time.

It was a female voice, from the same woman who had said "It's the time."

"I have been here for a long time already."

It was what it said.

"A long, long time. You know? Yes, you know it."

It sounded terrifying, full of hints. Thanks to the sewing machine, I would have been in serious trouble otherwise.

What had happened after we entered the village was leading me to the hell—the weird discomfort I had suffered, the strange voice message from a number that was non-existent, the laughter that on one but I had heard, the deafening noise that rocked the whole village, the wicked giggling from the backyard, and the white skirt and red shoes I saw a moment ago.

But the knock against the wall had wakened me up.

When I entered the room, I had been totally unaware of the sewing machine and hurt myself when I squatted down. It meant I was in an unusual state after the interference and was unable to concentrate and make independent judgments about the environment.

It had all started when I entered the "haunted house," as I had been feeling much more "comfortable." I had thought it was a sign that I was recovering physically, but I have been actually caught in the trap.

It could also be that I had been captivated by the earthbound spirit in *feng shui*. But if I had been possessed by the magic power, how was it possible for me to free myself by hitting my forehead on the sewing machine?

If I had nothing to do with a supernatural power, what had been influencing me must be the drug.

It was the smell that drifted in the house. It must be able to interfere with my process of reasoning and thinking. It might induce hallucinations at a higher dose. That had been why I went out of the room at once, even when no noise from the backyard was heard again.

That had helped me in my quick decision to go into the cellar. As the drug had been used to mislead me, what was waiting for me should not be death.

I took out my phone, but I could not see a tiny pool of dim light.

"Who's there?" I feigned a quivering voice, moving to the source of the noise.

"It's me. Don't you recognize my voice?"

It was a confusing question.

I continued, without answering it, until I reached it soon as it was only about five steps away.

It was from where the second or third basket lay on the shelf against the wall on my left.

The baskets for grapes were often small, to help the fruits at the bottom stay fresh. They were only big enough to hold a newborn baby … or the head of an adult.

Another sigh of relief was heard.

"Have you forgotten all about me?"

"Oh, no. Of course not."

"But why did you do it to me?"

I managed to locate the voice, but, strangely enough, it seemed it was not from an exact spot, but everywhere.

I suddenly felt an overwhelming desire to laugh, because of the tone it adopted.

If the house had been haunted, as the villagers believed, the spooks would be nobody but the mother and her daughter. It was most probable that it was the girl, because the two moving feet I had seen at the entrance of the cellar were meant to remind me of the girl, the last one who had disappeared. By the way, I had never thought about how they had made me believe it was a girl sitting at the opening. There could be numerous choices, but one simple way was to put the shoes on one's hands and a blouse over one's arms.

So, the voice had talked with me on the cellar should be the girl's spook.

But the voice I had heard just now was different.

If I was so confused that I was not able to see this contradiction now I would be a laughing stock to myself.

"No." I stopped myself. As I was still under the influence of the drug, most probably I would make a mistake. It was more important for me to follow what was going on before me.

I reached for another basket.

It was not heavy. I turned it over and the contents scattered about my feet.

I had not meant a person was in it, but I had guessed there might be a loudspeaker or something.

I bent over it. With the help of my flashlight, I saw clearly they were nothing else, but grapes, or raisins, to be exact, which looked nothing special from those dried in the sun. I knew I could never taste them. I checked the grapes with my foot, and I saw nothing buried in it.

I reached out for another basket.

When I held the third in my hand, the noise was heard again.

"Stop doing what're doing—it's all a waste of your effort."

Then she started to giggle.

The fit of giggles echoed in the cellar. It was obviously in front of me, but I could not see a soul with the help of the dim light.

It was not from any of the baskets, but the wall behind them. Yes, the base of the wall. It sounded as if it came from underground.

Well, even now I had an illusion that if I hadn't hit the wall …

Yes, when the sound came from behind the wall, it would be so diluted that it would hard for human ears to locate its source.

I raised my hand to check if it was a hollow wall by knocking at it, but I stopped in the middle.

It was dark here. An infra-red camera would be needed to monitor what was going on, but the power line would have to be connected all the way to a source in the village. So the monitor would be something elI was asked to stop what I was doing, because I had been heard scattering the grapes. If I was flustered in terror a moment ago, my action to knock at the wall meant I was very restrained. She must know that I had not fallen into her trap.

Sometimes, it was not wise to knock at a wall to see it was a hollow one.

Standing in silence, I thought about the structure of cellars for grapes. I knew about it, because I had seen how it was built when I was a small boy.

Yes, they must be thermally insulated structures, with walls with sawdust or cottonseed hulls stuffed in an inside space of twenty to thirty centimeters. More importantly, there must be vents for air, where small electronic devices could be placed.

"Can you see me? But I can see you. Finally, I see you, after so much effort."

I was shocked.

But in no time, my shock turned into anger.

"You can see me? How ridiculous! I've never tried to hide myself," I said to myself. "If you've worked yourself into frenzy plotting ways to kill me, why don't you just do it now? Are you going to defeat me spiritually before you destroy my body? Is an evil trial waiting for me? You want to defeat me first spiritually and then physically, so you can kill me twice?"

What a pity!

Remember when shepherds quarrel, the wolf has a winning game, I thought.

Death? I did not fear it. But I could only accept it when evidence, solid but not false evidence, was presented.

I had been wondering who among the four was the one I had been looking for, but now he or she came to me.

"Go ahead; you come out," I shouted.

Then I started to laugh.

It was not a silent laughter, but a loud, wild, derisive and hysterical laughter.

Of course, I was only feigning it, as if I was under the influence of the drug. As I laughed, memories of what had happened to me came flooding back and I found myself unable to stop.

It was downright ridiculous that I had started a writing career and so many people loved my books. It was downright ridiculous that I wore the jade all the time. It was downright ridiculous that I was afraid of revisiting Kashgar in the past years. It was downright ridiculous that I went to bed with a woman but I had had no idea whether she was you or not. Now you were trying to trap me, but had failed because of a dewing machine. I laughed.

"Come on. You come out. Why do you hide? Where have been all these years? In this cellar? In the baskets? Have you been seasoned like those grapes?"

I ran about wildly, pushing the baskets over one after another. The shelf in the middle was knocked down and fell down noisily, causing other shelves to totter and then fall. What the voice was saying was drowned in the loud noise.

"You want me to die? You want to kill me? Come on. Where have you been in these twelve years? Have you been under the Khan Palace to get ready to be reincarnated? Do you know how I have felt about it? You know nothing. Do you know what death is? Do you know what evil is? Do you think you've got a better idea about them now? Do you want …?"

A dull, dead thud was heard and I was interrupted.

A sudden silence fell over the cellar.

It sounded as if a person suffering from delirium fainted after hitting his head against a wall during one of his fits.

I was lying on the ground exhausted after my performance, twitching my arms and legs. With all my might, rushed over and hit the partition wall with my shoulder. It was not strong enough and I made a hole out of it, where crumbles and dust fell down. A terrible pain shot through my shoulder, and, I lay on the ground with my teeth clamping together, feigning death.

If I had been the monitor, I would have been desperately unhappy.

This was what had been expected to happen: the guy under the influence of the psychedelic drug would be frightened to death, so much so that he would even have hallucinations. The manipulated voice was purposely designed to change rhythmically as a means of brutal torture. The revenge was carefully planned, and much more would come.

Unfortunately, it sounded that I had got fainted or even had been dead.

If I fainted, I would recover from the influence of the drug when I woke up. So the best time to kill me would be before it.

What about if I was dead?

She would have to make sure that I was! She had restrained herself for years to prepare for this trap of hers. How could it possible for her to give it all up for her own safety? Even I myself as a writer with a twisted mind would not change my mind. Actually, the more twisted one's mind was, the further one would go at this crucial point in one's life, allowing no chance either for others or for oneself.

I lay myself flat on the ground. My face was against the dry grapes, which squirmed like little beetles. I thought I was still under the influence of the drug, but it would not matter much so long as I could still know right from wrong.

"You have vowed to take your revenge, but your heart, once a heart of gold, will be one of stone, more perverted than mine, when you're before me."

But I would not humor you.

I felt for my telephone on the ground. Holding it my hand, I lit the screen up. With the help of the faint light, I lifted up my head to crawl along on all fours. I could hear these beetles crushing under my weight.

"Rise to your feet.

Rise to your feet."

She shouted. Ignoring her, I crawled on, with great care so that I was not heard.

A fit of giggling was then heard.

Turned a deaf ear to it, I moved on.

"Do you still remember my name?

Have you forgotten it all?

What's wrong with you?"

With that, it did not speak any more.

Breathing slowly in and out, I went up the stairs slowly, until I reached the blocked entrance.

As I had expected, what blocked the entrance was a stone slab, which was the cover of the cellar that I had seen before. It must be as heavy as fifty kilos, but it could be removed manually. The stone had not been there to seal the opening permanently, but to keep the bright sunlight from entering the cellar for a closed independent space. Theoretically, I would have gone so raving mad under the influences of the drug and the mysterious voice that I would manage to escape by pushing the slab away.

But I did not even touch the stone, but waited in silence.

For open sesame.

For the truth.

For the end.

I crouched against the wall, listening to my own breathing. I breathed slowly in and out, but it seemed the sound came from somewhere else. Then I heard the beat of my heart. The breathing was like wind, and heart thumps were like a clap of thunder. They were amplified in my ears, blowing up like a storm.

It was almost like a nightmare. I managed to concentrate to struggle free when I realized a different sound mingled with it.

I was phone ringing.

Suddenly, the wind and the thunder died.

It was Zhong Yi.

"F--k!"

"Pick it up?"

"No!"

"The monitors would react to the movement of my phone? No, they are unable to identify in which direction a voice comes, which put me at ease."

The phone kept shrilling furiously, for such a long time that I was becoming increasingly agitated.

Suddenly a deafening noise of rumble was heard before dust fell down. The stone plate was moving. Who is out there?

A tiny crack of light was seen, and it was becoming wider and wider, until it was blocked by a figure before it was seen again.

"I don't give a damn who it is." My fears and anxieties came back again.

Taking a deep breath, I jumped to push the stone away with my shoulder. As soon as I was out, I flattened her on the ground by holding her neck with my right hand.

I felt as if the sky and the earth were rotating around me, and the dazzling sunlight, soil, grass and houses flashed before me, until my eyes fixed on a human face.

Before I could see who it was, I was hit with a stick on the face.

I was pitched onto the road. My ears were humming and tingling and they became hot and tense, but I didn't feel any pain. I was lying on my back in bright sunshine, too weak to move.

A face appeared above me, and it was the woman who I had seized by the throat. Now I could see it was Zhong Yi.

She looked at me, and then turned to scream at Fan Sicong,

who dropped her stick with embarrassment.

"Terribly sorry. Sicong didn't see it was you when you charged out. We've been looking for you for ages, but why didn't you answer us? Why were you down there?"

Staring at her through my lashes, I ran my tongue in my mouth before I spat out my back tooth. I smiled at her.

"Thanks," I said.

Chapter VII In the Desert

Something made one move in the shadow.

It was a lizard, as long as a human finger. It would be a moving green reptile in the sun, but now it was too dark to see it clearly. In a deft movement, it disappeared in the shade of the rose willows. It might be a scorpion, too. Yuan Ye drilled into us that it was dangerous to make our way through willow forests along the road and into the desert, because they were home to this poisonous creature.

We were more than two hundred kilometers into Taklimakan desert. I was waiting for Zhong Yi.

A voice had been whispering into my ear, but I but couldn't make out what it was saying. It had been heard ever since we came to the first village in Luobu. It would disappear when I listened hard, as if it was generated in my mind. Was it a mosquito with a woman's face? Buzzing, buzzing, humming, humming.

It might be the leftover of the hit on the head—I was slightly concussed?

So I became a bit daffy. I kicked over the wooden armchair when I came out of the haunted house with my hands over my head. The lower part of the chair was rather different, with four boards between the legs on each side. Once it lay on the ground, we could see what was at the bottom—glowing ash.

"Marijuana?" I turned to Fan Sicong and then Zhong Yi and smiled. "The chair might have been burned."

Zhong Yi bent down at once to examine it. You could begin to hallucinate like me, I told her. Then I patted her on the shoulder, saying you smelled of blood.

She straightened herself up immediately to stare at me, with a weird air on her face.

"I probably have inhaled too much marijuana," I said.

"The blood on the leaf may be from a man."

I had a turn of dizziness and a splitting headache, and I had lost the ability to think rationally. Fortunately, I had managed to free myself from the trap. When I stumbled out of the house, Chen Ailing, who was waiting for me outside, got a terrible shock and asked me what had happened. Patting my face with my hands, I turned to ask where the other two had been.

"Why did you ask us?" Fan Sicong said, clearly annoyed. "Tell us why you entered the cave and how it was covered with stone."

I gave him a dirty look. "Why did you get separated from Zhong Yi?"

He was taken aback, unable to speak, but Zhong Yi was quick enough to say that they had been together.

I smiled mockingly and pressed Fan Sicong. "Have you?"

He said "yes," but in an unusually weak voice.

What was he afraid of? Was he laying to me? I turned to Zhong Yi, who was eyeing Fan Sicong, with a veiled hint on her face.

Chen Ailing suggested that I rest in the car as quickly as possible. Walking out of the village, Zhong Yi asked how I knew about the ash at the bottom of the armchair.

"I knew nothing about it, but I saw a little girl was on it, with a white skirt and red shoes."

My answer silenced everyone.

With everyone seating in the car, we started our journey into the desert.

The car bumped along, and I was beginning to feel a little faint. As I was unable to concentrate, I tried to sleep. But I knew what I was going to do.

When the car stopped for us to relieve ourselves, I was awakened and asked Yuan Ye if everybody was around when the car was repaired after dinner. He told me Fan Sicong and Zhong Yi were away for quite a long time. Asked about the problem with the tire after our convenience supper, he said it had a puncture, but it would have been a slow one if the nail was still inside it. He guessed that the tire had been tampered with because the hole was found in an unusual place.

When asked where he was when the vehicle was repaired and whether he was with Zhong Yi, what would Fan Sicong say? Would he insist that he hadn't been separated from her?

It was me who raised the subject of Luobu community, but earlier Zhong Yi had talked to Fan Sicong about the Luobu village for tourists.

As she knows me rather well, did she ever guess that I intended to start on the topic of the local village by making fun of Fan Sicong? I thought.

Yes, it's possible.

I had to admit that I was misled. As forces are mutual, I was easily calculated when I tried to disturb Fan Sicong. I had thought it was my choice to go to the local community, but it was her design.

She must know much about the village, the haunted house and even the cellar. This was the battle field she had chosen.

I was also wondering how I could fall asleep when the car was repaired. I couldn't understand why I suddenly felt bone tired. As marijuana could be placed in the house, it could be possible that sleeping pills could have been put in my food.

She could have enough time to prepare for it in the hours when I was asleep. As we had been together since we set out, she must need the time to be left alone.

Did Fan Sicong's changed tone of voice and expression on

his face show his curiosity about it? If Zhong Yi managed to find a valid excuse for leaving him, he must be wondering what she had done in those hours and in the house. However, a humble, ordinary-looking young man would naturally take the side of the woman of his dreams.

Or they could be conspirators?

He got involved in it because he was not happy with me?

Yes, no, yes ... I could hear a voice was whispering in my ear. I kept my eyes closed with my hands holding my head when a horn blared in front of me. I opened my eyes and saw a shadowy figure moving over in two beams of light.

Before me were car headlights on full beam.

It was Zhong Yi, who was courageous enough to come over.

She came in Yuan Ye's car. It was dark in the vehicle, but I thought he glanced at me as he drove away. Did he do it for himself or was he curious about my relationship with Zhong Yi? He may be thinking that I could help him because I had been popular with women.

What he did not know was that my heart was filled with indomitable ill will at the moment.

Did Zhong Yi know it? She must since she was a clever woman and knew me so well.

I stayed alone in a house in the desert.

It was the house for a caretaker, one of the more than a hundred houses along the highway through the desert, which stretched several hundred kilometers. The caretakers lived there with their wives. Each of them was responsible for watering several kilometers of grass and shrubs, which helped keep sand away from the road.

We had planned to spend the night in the desert town, but the western side of the only hotel was being renovated and more than half of its rooms were not available for guests. There was only one room left for us when we made our reservation. Fortunately, the man at the hotel helped us to contact the highway caretakers, who offered their houses to us for extra money. The houses were more expensive, and we rented three of them. Chen Ailing and I stayed alone and Fan Sicong and Yuan Ye shared one house. Zhong Yi stayed in the town hotel.

"Come in." I pulled the door open.

It seemed it was a temporary house, but the walls were made of concrete. The bulb dangling from the ceiling gave out a murky light, and the electricity came from a small diesel generator in the back yard.

I had had a nap in the car after supper, and we were already in the desert when I woke up. As my headache began to wear off, I started to think about what I would do next. As Chen Ailing got out first and then Fan Sicong, Zhong Yi was left alone with Yuan Ye, the driver, when I left the car. It was then I invited her.

"I think I have to talk to you," I recall saying.

"Okay, but I'm rather tired. I'll put my luggage in place first." Zhong Yi did not reject my suggestion out of hand, leaving me wondering when she would come.

I thought she wouldn't come when I waited for her by the roadside.

The road maintenance worker's house was a two-roomed unit with a square table and chairs in the outer room and a bed in the other, the only pieces of furniture in it.

I sat at the table, with Zhong Yi on the opposite side. It was the first time we seated ourselves so formally.

"I'm curious why none of you asked me on the way about what I had seen," I said.

"We did, but you didn't answer."

"Really?" I touched my head. "The hit from Fan Sicong has been deeply damaging to me."

She withdrew her hands from the top the table. It was the third time she replaced her hands, but it seemed she felt uneasy wherever they were.

I stood up and walked around for half of a round, seeing her clasped hands in front of her belly.

Slowly I moved to stand behind her, my body pressing hers,

but I could see her hands. Her long fingers seemed bloodlessly pale after her work with her luggage. Her fingernails were well-manicured and covered with flesh-colored nail polish.

"Much of your nail polish has worn off," I said abruptly. "Was it rubbed off this afternoon? That piece of rock had sharp edges. You're quite tough. Your hands are too delicate for the heavy work."

"Fan Sicong got the rock out of our way. I was not strong enough, you know. My polish doesn't stay well. It started to wear off several days ago."

"I see."

She turned to look at me, and I leaned down to touch her face with mine. I put my hand on her right arm and moved it down her sleeve.

She got goose bumps on her neck, which looked rather stiff.

"Does it hurt you?" I asked.

"What?"

"Or is it on this hand?" I patted her on her left arm.

"What are you talking about?"

"The wound, I mean," I sniffed.

"I could smell blood. Where is the cut?" I ran my hand across her outer thigh. "Is it on your leg? It's not visible, but it hurts you when you move."

She could not help shuddering and pushed my hand away.

"What are you doing? You smell blood because I've got my period."

Taken by surprise, I stepped back.

She rose in a fit of anger. "Why the hell did you asked me over here?"

I resumed my seat and smiled at her.

"Do you still remember the appointment we made yesterday, my psychologist?"

"Of course, I do. But it was something different when you put your filthy paws on me and was being sarcastic."

"I'm not able to think normally today. You know I was hit

by a stick on the head. Do you really remember what happened to me? I don't think you look like a psychologist since you are with me."

My words were met with a silence, before a sudden smile flickered across her face. "What do you think I look like?" she asked, taking her seat again.

"But it seems you are," I replied.

"Well, you want me to imagine that to jolt your memory?"

"No." I tapped my own head. "The hit has brought back some of the memory about it."

Staring at Zhong Yi, I could sense her nervousness, although she tried to hide it.

I determined to make her even more nervous.

"It was a hand, a left hand," I continued quietly and calmly. "It was covered with fine wrinkles, as if scratched on a peddle wall. The wrinkles were brown and filled with dirt that could never be removed. The fingers were rather short, and the pinkie was twisted, pointing like the barrel of a pistol. His fingernails cut into his flesh, and under his nails was dirt that could be places for earthworms. The part of the forearm near the hand was hairy, looking as if he had an old band around his wrist, but he had lost his hair on the rest of the arm probably because of his age. Muscles were still visible on the arm, but the skin was weathered, as if it was something hanging loosely on him. The veins stand out on the back of his hands, as if snakes trying to enter his body.

"His neck was terribly long and covered with wrinkles that were as fine as those in her hand. Actually, he was wrinkled all over; his skin would be twice as large when it was spread out on the floor. He was covered with dirt, as he seldom took a bath. When he did it, he would only wet himself, which would help the dirt stay longer. His skin sometimes would delude people into thinking that it was born blotchy and that it was covered with thicker cuticles. He had a dark hairy birthmark on his neck. The hairs were shiny and much longer than those on the back of his hands. With the dirt under them, they grew well. They must have small roots which sucked blood from under the skin.

"He had a pointed chin with a wispy beard, although he was hairy in other parts of his body and he never shaved. His beard was often seen to cling to his face or sometimes to his neck because it was always sticky with things like sheep fat or soaked in dribble. He had no ear lobe on his left ear; the scar told that it must have been bitten off by a person or dog. His hair was so bushy that it could be a place for many things, but it smelt like rotten meat. He had a pockmarked face with aging spots, which showed he had become a weak and flabby old man. His nose was strong and straight, but it seemed his face was sunken, looking like a dented pit between his high cheekbones, where his eyeballs, nose and lips were too badly decomposed to be identified.

"He wore a black suit and its cuffs had lost their shapes because the sleeves were often rolled up. Under it was a T-shirt with vertical stripes, which showed a lock of chest hair. It seemed her body hair had worked off all her energy, leaving her rather vulnerable to attack. The loose skin under his chest hair was so pallid that his bony ribs were clearly seen, as if they would crack with a punch."

I stared at Zhong Yi as I spoke. She wore a smile on her face, but it seemed a forced smile as her lips were becoming bloodless. Then she averted her eyes from my face.

My unusual pleasure, dull pain in my head, and a low humming sound in my ears mingled together and turn into an addiction, which gave forth an almost intoxicating scent.

"Below his ribs was a pyramid, an embedded pyramid, and the stupid belly button was like an entrance, leading to a grave. His gray stomach moves slowly up and down, looking as if maggots would come out anytime. They did come out, one after another, and buzzing flies ..."

"Enough," she murmured. Her voice was so tiny that I did know what she was saying, but I thought it was what she meant.

"You don't want me to continue?"

"Are you talking about a dead man?"

"Yes, he was dead. You knew it."

Zhong Yi had her head down, as if an ostrich who was trying burying its head in sand. The last few words of mine sent a subtle shudder through her.

Leaning forward, I saw in front of her clasped hands in front of her belly, which showed taut muscles and bulging veins.

The wind whistled for a minute outside the window. She said something, but I didn't hear what she said because of the wind. Then it seemed she had made a decision. She relaxed her arms and raised her head, and then she repeated the action.

"Why?"

"Why did you do it?"

Her voice was becoming louder. She resumed what she really was, knowing it would be useless to continue to pretend otherwise.

"Welcome back, my goddess," I said. "You have too many questions to ask, even when you know what the answers are."

"He has been there for ages," she replied with a weird smile. "But nobody has ever discovered him."

"He was only one of the thousands of people buried in the past hundreds of years in a labyrinth of tunnels under the ground. Don't worry about him. He was not lonely there."

"I could never understand why you killed. Tell me your reason in doing so." She eyed me nastily, as if in warning.

"Why I killed him or you?" I began to laugh. "You're lying. You are lying."

I rose slowly, put my hands on the desk, and looked into her eyes.

"All you need is my reason for that? You did all that only for the reason? You've been working really hard."

She was on her way to rise but leaned back to make room for me, which caused her to fall down along with the chair.

Simultaneously, light came in a pool on the ground and two impatient horns blasted outside.

She sprang to her feet in the matter of a second.

"It's Yuan Ye coming for me," she said.

It was his car outside. In a time as short as half an hour, she made an appointment with him for picking her up.

"You've mistaken me for someone else," she said when passing me. "I'm Zhong Yi, not the guy you want. Was what you said just now what you did? Were you really the killer?"

"Hey Zhong Yi." I called to her when she opened her door.

She turned her head.

"Good night," I said.

"It will be a find day tomorrow," she said, casting a glance up at the sky.

I watched her walk out, get into Yuan Ye's car, and disappear from view.

She moved in unsteady steps, with a weakness in her legs.

Turning off the light, I stood at the window, waiting for Yuan Ye's car to pass my room again before I headed to Tazhong town.

Chapter VIII Boomerang

I felt numb all over with cold as I walked across the desert in the windy night.

The road was bathed in the moonlight, glinting weirdly. It went rolling as if it stretched endlessly. I had left two sand dunes behind me, and I expected to see Tazhong beyond the two or three ahead me.

"How did I deal with Zhong Yi's body? What a problem!"

A throbbing in the head.

Maybe I didn't have a concussion. Maybe I have a cold?

Another slope was before me.

The last drops of blood—dark red blood—oozed slowly. The murderer cut off the nose cleanly first, because it was prominently straight, sharp, and pointed. Enduring the sharp pain, he kept his eyes wide open to see who the murderer was, but his eyes were gouged out. The unskillful murderer burst the left eyeball, unable to take it out as a whole, leaving the broken lens in place, but the right one was removed. My story "Write from Memory" tells how a person is dismembered alive.

But it is fictional.

What I actually did first with my knife was to remove the birthmark? I remembered I did it. It was the one on the neck, with hair on it. I did it for the same reason—it had been an eyesore for me, for as long as five years.

All forms of fiction have truth as a source.

When I retrieved my knife, I saw blood spurting like water in a spring. No, it was rather like the rough sea.

As I was approaching the crest of the slope, I could see the whole of the curving slope, which led to Tazhong.

It was not as far as I had predicted. I was unable to estimate accurately every time, just as what had happened to the Luobu community. But it was good enough if I could choose what was right when I had to.

"What can I do with her body?"

I walked down the way, and a truck passed with its high beams on. I turned my face away to avoid the driver.

How is it that I can remember what happened years ago. The scenes flashed my mind one after another like a boomerang and I recalled more. Was I nervous because I hadn't killed anyone in the past? Of course not, I had been a writer of stories, and with every story I reviewed what I had experienced. It was like a military exercise, where first-personal shooting games were used to train pilots and shooters.

I had imagined numerous times that I was cutting off the birthmark. But it was only the first step. I had to pick off the hairs on it wisp by wisp, although with blood they were too slippery to handle.

I talked to him for a long time. As what happens in my stories, crazed killers chat with dead bodies. "I had long hoped to remove those hairs. Do you still remember I told you something like this? Now you see it doesn't hurt when I pick them off. You told me how to do it, didn't you? You tapped my pinkie with a hammer when my stomach griped, and the pain began to wear off. But unlike yours, my finger recovered. Were you disappointed?"

How did he react? A coward, he was too scared to speak, with nothing on. It must hurt a lot, because he lost a lot of blood, pools of blood.

"I hate you," I told him.

He seemed to talk again, to moan, to be exact. It upset me. And I cut him again, across his lips, but it was not deep enough to cut through them. "Stop crying," I warned him. "It would break your mouth." Yes, it was exactly what I had written in one of my story. Fiction has truth as its source, right?

Then I rambled on to him. What else could I do? I had to tell him why I did what I had done to him.

Actually, they were not related to each other—what I needed was nothing but a long talk. I told him he was a man in my life, who I could never forget easily. I removed the second knuckle in his right index finger. It was the hardest part in his body, which hurt me most when he beat me. Well, I told this story in one of my books, with the following dialogue:

"You're a dirty guy. I thought what is inside is black, but it's red. When I cut deeper into it, it becomes white. Whatever color it is, it's dirty. I don't give a damn if you treat me shabbily, refuse to give me my share of the money, or hate it when I'm with her. What do you think I care most?"

When I finished, his mouth had been cut into something looking like a flower. Even if he had the strength to grumble, it would be impossible for me to understand what he was saying.

"What I care most about is that you're dirty," I told him frankly. "I wanted to make you cleaner, but I'm not skillful enough. I cut you in a random way, and I'm not quick enough."

He would die soon, in the view of contemporary medicine. But as muscles are more active than the brain, his flesh shivered as my knife came in and out.

She was with me when I did all this, but when and how did she leave?

My head began to hurt me.

I walked along the way to the town. She would never be able to get away with it this time.

I wondered how she had the guts to come to me again. I would never bother to look for her if she had had disappeared from my sight. Actually, I had almost forgotten all about her. I thought I had been dead.

For years I had been convinced that she was dead, because she had never turned up. Why hadn't she come to avenge or report it to the police? Ten years had passed, so she had been dead and it was me who killed her. She was unable to escape and survive it. Yes, she was dead.

I had thought I could only meet her in my stories. She, he, and me.

Over the years, numerous people had been murdered in my work. Their heads were severed from their bodies, their noses were lopped off, their eyes were removed, and sometimes they were raped in a perverted manner. For example, the teeth of Azhi in "The Millstone" were knocked out before her body was shaped into a flying Apsaras like the frescoes of the Dunhuang caves. No one in my work die a natural death. And the murderers—some of them were filled with hate, some were lascivious and insatiable, and some were simply waiting for a glimpse of death.

I had been writing about myself, which I had known quite well from the very beginning.

I realized that I was a gold mine that night twelve years ago. When I wrote, I was digging up treasure. Every story of mine was an account of what had happened in the past. Of course, it had to be part of the event. I smashed myself to pieces and put them on a board for close examination. I had never understood what I was. Every time a story was finished, I regretted that the pieces were not tiny enough to be bite-sized, but my readers felt I was already unspeakably cruel.

I told them that only killers knew what killers were.

I was lying, as I didn't know what I myself was.

Maybe she knew me more, the lovely figure which had a lucky escape under my knife.

I am not sure what really happened to me in those five years, not because I'm forgetful but because I remembered more than I can manage. The scenarios overlap, but they are different from each other and even contrast sharply, as if the world had forked as the pool of blood formed.

It was because I thought I had recalled too much of the past and written too many books. My stories, which resembled more or less my memories of the past, had gradually become part of my personal life. They were like repeated strokes of paint on a canvas, leaving the first color nowhere to be seen.

I had thought she had been dead in a painting.

It turned out that she was about to die soon.

It was a small town, so small that it had only one road. It was the one that I had taken to come. The town was by the road, and on the other side was the desert.

Along the road was a gas station, a store, a bingo hall, a KTV, and several massage parlors, where drivers could have sex. It was a place where drivers could get sufficiently refreshed and relaxed during their long journeys.

Among them was also an inn, where I had stayed ten years ago when it was newly-built.

It was 1:20 in the morning. I walked along on the desert side of the road, to avoid the warm light from the massage parlors. The sex workers could only see a moving figure when they looked in my direction.

The inn door was open, and I could see the faint light inside. I walked along the carriageway to the back yard. The open door was what I had been.

It was a small door about 1.4 meters high. I stooped down to go in. Before me was a staircase, which lead to the reception desk, where no one was seen.

Going up the stairs, I heard the noises from a television on the first floor, but it was rather quiet on the second.

I had no idea where her room was, but I guessed it was on the top floor as it was the last one available for her. The last occupied rooms were always the most unwelcome ones. In a hotel without an elevator, the higher floors were not preferred.

It must be on the second floor.

With sacks of cement and boards on the corridor on the right, I knew some construction was underway. I turned left.

The lights over my head kept flickering, making a low humming sound. Looking around, I was pleased that there was no camera on the wall.

The corridor was not carpeted and the concrete floor was shining. There were fourteen rooms, with seven on each side. Which one was hers?

I went down, with my hands and knees on the floor like a dog. Lowering my head until my nose reached the floor, I began to smell around.

I did it to scent blood.

I scratched the blood-clotted wound on my forehead when I took out the luggage from the trunk. With my blood on the wheels of her bag, she went into her room on the third floor, leaving behind her a trail of smell, which became so faint in a dusty environment after a couple of hours that only a dog could sense it. The animal had a nose that was far more sensitive than ours, being able to identify hundreds of scents that were beyond human ability. I was not that good at all with smells, but I do well in picking up the smell of blood.

I moved around the corridor before I rose to my feet.

Room 315.

I flicked away the dust on my gloves, unzipped my bag and took out a knife, a bit of wire, and a tough alloy cable, a cord of three strands of different qualities. After I placed the bag against a wall, I fastened the knife with its scabbard to my back under my belt, casually wrapped the cable around my forearm while holding one of its ends in my hand, and twisted the wire.

When all was ready, I took off the silk glove on my right hand and inserted the wire in my bare hand into the lock.

I hated to touch dirty things with my hands, but I knew sometimes I had to. I tried to imagine that the distinct uneasiness I felt when my hands contacted the outside world was a nothing but a special pleasure.

I took off my silk gloves so that I could easily fasten the wire tighter and without making much noise.

I did it.

I turned the handle and pushed at the door. I stopped immediately when it creaked open. It was not at all noisy, but I heard it more than clearly. The door opened a crack, so I could see it was dark inside. But the light from the corridor filtered into it.

I put the wire back into my pocket and put on my gloves. It was still quiet in the room.

I twisted the alloy in my left hand, and began to push at the door again.

The second noise was heard much later than I had expected, and the door creaked open an inch.

Hearing no noise inside, I poked my head in to listen.

I was expecting the familiar breathing, but I heard the damning buzzing sound in my own head, which seemed to be always there. Damn it—my head hurt me again.

Buzz, buzz, buzz.

I walked in.

The light fell in a pool at the end of the bed. I frowned as I closed the door behind me and turned the light on.

It was empty.

Looking around, I realized quickly that the room had not been used.

Am I in a wrong room? I must have mistaken the room for hers, because the smell of the blood was so faint.

Where is her room? I forgot to leave a mark in front of it. It was impolite to wake the attendant up for it.

I had to wait.

Her reservation was the last room available. Where could it be?

I glanced around the room again. It seemed the sheets on the bed had not been used, and the table was clean, with cups in their place. Yes, it had not been used.

I went into the toilet. The toothbrush bag remained intact, the toilet seat was in place, and a used sanitary pad was seen in the basket nearby.

She was gone!

Life is like a story, an intriguing story like the ones that I write.

Nothing can be done with unexpected ease.

I stared at my face in the bathroom mirror for a long while before I dragged my backpack into the toilet to repack my knife, alloy cable and wire. I fished out a small leather case out of the bag, in which I had my full of odds and ends.

After I disguised myself with a wig, a false beard, a pair of glasses with dark thick frames, and a tube of dark face cream, I emptied the bag and shook it inside out, turning the black backpack into a white shoulder bag.

For years, I had never forgotten where I came from, all ready to be forced to be what I had been.

There were quite a number of cars parking around the gas station. The hotels were packed with guests, and many tourists had to spend the night in the cars.

When I woke him up, a guy sleeping on the back seat in a black Volkswagen was obviously deeply upset, but his face glowed when he saw with the help of his torch what I had in my hand was a thick wad of notes.

Weighing carefully the possible danger of a guest who rent his car at night, he decided to risk it for the four thousand yuan. It turned out he was travelling in the same direction, but I had to leave a couple of hours earlier.

I told him I had to catch the early flight with the made-up

excuse about a family member's severe illness. Without a word, he started the car and headed towards Luntai. He attempted to begin a conversation by saying quite a number of people rented his car tonight. Thinking he was talking about Zhong Yi, I kept silent, not trying to ask what car she was in and if it was headed for Mingfeng or Luntai. Instead, I said I needed a nap, which silenced him.

It was not hard for me to know where Zhong Yi was travelling. The nearest airport in the direction of Minfeng was Hetian, which was three hundred kilometers farther than Kuerla, the airport in the direction of Luntai. Wasn't it stupid of a woman who managed to escape with her life had chosen the farther one? Or even when she had chosen not to fly, she would have a better access to public transportation in North Xinjiang than in South Xinjiang. On the other side of the Taklamakan Desert was Mingfeng, a typical southern town, where few Han people lived and she would face more danger. All evidence pointed to her choice of Luntai.

The car she was in was the only incoming vehicle, a truck that I had seen when I was on the road. I could catch up to it before I reached Luntai, as the car was much faster.

Sitting in the back seat with my eyes half-open, I stared at the dark desert land, but I saw her face. It was a face different from Zhong Yi's, looking much younger. I could hardly see the face, but I felt I saw her, clearly.

I saw she had her head on the shoulder of the old man, her silky skin against the hairy birthmark. She was so pure that she looked like an angel in paradise, looking deceptively gentle. Gathering no dust or sand, her skin was glistening under the morning sun. Every time I saw her touching the dirty, mud-covered man, I thought it was all an illusion, something that was patently absurd. Any thought about it made me physically sick. When he put his hand on her, I felt as if a dog was gnawing at my face or my heart. The beast had a face like his and worked with his dirty, broken teeth and wet tongue.

I had been tortured like this for five years, and it was all my own fault.

I had been dreaming to become a legendary jade miner, following the steps of my father and grandfather. I would not hesitate even a second even if I had to be unlucky to die young, as they had been. As a pop song put it, "I longed for nothing but to leave home to travel to far places." When I met the old man, a jade miner, on a scorching summer day, I spoke in a bombastic way about how good I was at jade mining, to which I added the stories of my father and grandfather. When he told me he would take me away, I almost jumped in surprise, as if a strong wind coming from nowhere helped me on a journey to a distinguished career as a jade miner.

She was with him. She was an angel on Earth. When she came to me, all my troubles and difficulties vanished instantly from my mind, like snow under the sun.

As I travelled to more places, I understood that the stories of my father and grandfather had spread far beyond my hometown. All jade dealers of older generations knew something about them. The old man was no exception. That was why he believed what a teenager said and took the stranger with him. He thought I or my family would bring him good luck. My grandfather had been lucky enough to own a piece of white jade as large as thirteen kilos, and my father nearly stumbled over a rare yellow jade of six kilos. It would be a great deal for him, if it happened that I was as lucky as they were, even if there was only a million-to-one chance of it happening.

What happened later proved that he was right.

But I did not realize when we first met how evil and dirty he was. He could turn any innocent person into the most depraved one, including her.

Help must be offered before degeneration.

I thought I would catch up with her before dawn.

I missed her so much that I longed to talk to her, so I felt for my phone. All of a sudden, I realized that I did not have my gloves on. I had removed them at the hotel when I put on my wig and false whiskers. I had put them in my bag after I rolled them up, but I had forgotten to put on a new pair, which was a mistake I seldom made.

While I wrote stories these years, I read many books on psychology. I had tried to understand why I picked up the habit of wearing gloves. This obsession about cleanliness, which I had been in the grip of rather late in my life, must have to do with the hatred flaring up inside me towards the dirty old man. It had been getting worse over the years that I felt nothing in the world was clean. Was she still clean as she had been after so many years?

But I had no gloves on my hands!

To my great surprise, I felt nothing over it. Great! I had fully recovered from the illness.

I took out my phone to text her.

"Asleep? Your room number? I want to come over for a chat."

I waited with interest for her message, hoping it would be a sideshow in my journey.

My phone went dim, as its battery was running low. I wondered if I had succeeded in sending the message. I hadn't had the time to recharge my phone. The batteries on smart phones did not last, but it seemed mine worked for even a shorter time today.

The world around me fell silent.

The pop songs in the local language continued, the engine was running, and the vehicles rushed past me, but the world fell silent for me.

I guessed it was an illusion.

Actually, it was not a moment of silence, but a moment of tranquility.

I was numbed for a while, before I realized it was that noise that I could no longer hear.

It had been an extremely faint sound, as if an invisible man was grinding his teeth in my ear, but I could hear it. It had been torturing me for nearly ten hours since I entered the village, but it vanished a moment ago.

A person who walks around with sandbags wrapped on his legs would get used to their weight, but when the bags are removed, he would feel he is as light as a feather, as if he would float in the wind. The noise had been like a sand bag in my mind. I could see how my mind had been in a whirl only when the noise disappeared.

My eyes were on the dead phone.

Yes, it was all on account of the phone.

The awful noise was from my phone.

It must be a high-pitched sound, with a frequency that challenges human hearing range so that it seemed to come and go, being terribly unpleasant.

As the hacker had easy access to my computer, she could have hacked into my cell phone system. To make it worse, she had been with me these days, working closely together. All that had happened later started from a sudden noise, which was a much better weapon than those tricky plays such as pretending to be a ghost and burning the cannabis plants. The noise had left me dazed and unable to concentrate, alluring me step by step into her snare and almost ruined me.

In no time I had realized why I had failed in striking back in the cellar. There was a loudspeaker behind the wall, but a receiver was needed to make me heard outside. As my phone had been invaded to make it an ideal receiver, they were able to monitor what I was doing. My phone had betrayed me when I thought I could make her believe that I had fainted from a hit on the wall as I was crawling along on my belly.

My cell phone failed me today. Its batteries had worn out quickly because it was used so often.

The very review of what I had done, including my conversation with her, brought me out in a cold sweat.

My words and behavior had been different, simply because I

was mentally disturbed without my knowledge. When I thought about it now, I regretted, regretted, regretted.

I was most clear-headed than I ever was since I started the trip. It was as if I had a beacon in my mind, its blinking moving slowly over a dark sea so that I could see how the waves rose and fell.

What I first saw was that she was not alone.

While the car was fixed, she left with Fan Sicong; in the ghost room, they were together, too. She must have first left to get ready, which may include buying the clothes for girls and placing the voicing device in the cellar, and then she needed the time to talk to me when I was struggling in the cellar. I had thought she must need an excuse to be alone to avoid being seen by Fan Sicong. And Fan Sicong may have become suspicious of her motives, but chose to be silent because of his love for her.

But the noise led me to a big mistake. If she had been the only person behind all this, she needed to leave Fan Sicong three times, not two.

I had forgotten about the cannabis plants!

They had been burning for quite a while when I entered the ghost room. When did she light them up?

Chen Ailing and I walked in front when we first entered the village. Fan Sicong and her lagged behind, but soon they took a side path. It took them quite a while to join us again. It must be during this time when the cannabis plants started to burn.

An absence could be a perfect excuse, two will make Fan Sicong suspicious, and three were impossible, unless he was put in a trance.

Fan Sicong must be in cahoots with her!

But why did she escape alone?

Wait, there must be someone else!

I had heard someone laughing from behind after I received that voice message. Fan Sicong denied hearing it, because he was on her side, but why did Chen Ailing also deny it?

"Did you hear anything? It was terrible, but it was gone." I asked the driver, unexpectedly.

"You awake? Seemed I heard some noise. I thought it was my illusion. I don't know what that sound was. Yes, it's gone. How weird!"

I had asked Chen Ailing about the terrible noise, when she had been as near to me as the driver in a much quieter environment. She told me "No."

As a representative from the company, why would Chen Ailing mingle with her?

Oh.

It was her who told me that Chen Ailing was from the company, Zhong Yi was from the advertiser, Fan Sicong was the cameraman, and I was invited to join the journey along the Silk Road, but I had never checked it. No one would check it. I had never thought about doing it for the dozens of similar commercial activities I was involved in.

What about Yuan Ye? Yes and no. He looked like nothing else but a driver. He would remain silent if not asked, probably thinking it must be an illusion.

Well, behind all this was not one guy or two guys, but all of them in the group, something I had never expected!

What I realized next was that this was just her.

Revenge was often undertaken by a single person, because one guy's revenge was seldom shared by another, who could not feel the same pain. In addition, people who vowed to take their revenge often had something in their mind that they found hard to disclose. If Zhong Yi had been the woman involved in the crime at the time, why had Chen Ailing and Fan Sicong been trying to help her? It would be unusual for anyone to put themselves into the path of a murderer. A safer way would be to report it to the police.

What had happened in the cellar was good proof.

I had felt then something was wrong, but I had not given it

a second thought. The guy had appeared as the ghost of the girl to frighten the life out of me. This had been superfluous, only to find it had led to a logical contradiction: it was her who "made her presence as the ghost." Of course, she had nothing to do with the little girl. But why would they "made their presence" at the same time? It would not be serious enough for the two to be possessed by the same ghost. This reasoning showed the presence of the girl was neither natural nor necessary. To frighten me, she should have done it all by herself.

How could the trap setter have made this stupid logical error? It could only be that she had had no other choice, but frighten me with the girl, because she knew nothing at all about what had happened.

This was not just her.

Zhong Yi was Zhong Yi. She might have adopted a different name, but she was not the other one, who must have a face, a body, and body odor of her own. She had not had perfect plastic surgery done—they were simply not the same person.

I was haunted.

She should have been dead … and it should be me who did it.

I closed my eyes, to review quickly what she had said in the cell.

She had been wringing something out of me!

The speaking woman actually knew nothing. She had been wringing something out of me.

How had they managed a situation like that?

I remembered her terribly pale face when she left last night. What had she asked before leaving? She asked when it would take place if I had arranged everything in my stories. What had I told her? I remembered telling her I had to think about it.

Damn it. What a fool I had been!

My reaction would allow her to see how vital her question was and what a loaded question it was. It meant I did believe that someone had been against me, which, in turn, meant I had committed a sin of some type. It also meant I had been holding things back, which would help me to come to a sensible conclusion. Zhong Yi was finally convinced that I believed someone had vowed to take her revenge on me and that I knew why the guy had been with us.

She was frightened out of her wits!

She disguised herself as the guy who had been seeking revenge, to worm the secret out of me.

As it was not Zhong Yi, the guy was already dead, and no one else except me knew what had happened, it should be clear to me that the encrypted files in my computer had not been created as a ceremony of death, which I had thought to be. Instead, they were designed to hook me and to motivate my memory, leading me all the way to Kashgar, the destination, where I would be brought to trial to satisfy their urge for revenge.

I took out my laptop, switched it on, inserted my flash disk, and double clicked on the two files in code—"In Hetian" and "In Kashgar."

I tried a couple of passwords. Finally, I succeeded.

The code for the first story, "In Hetian," was the date when I woke up under the tree and for the second file, "In Kashgar," was the number of days for which I had lost my memory. I had made up the story that I woke up under the tree, and I had never lost my memory. I had tried the digits of the date when the crime was committed and the days I had been in the wild, but not those two false digits. I had thought it was an act of revenge for my crimes, so I had never considered those meaningless numbers. It turned out that the author of the four stories had been totally ignorant about it.

I had a quick scan through the two stories. Just like the other two, they were murder cases which had nothing to do with me.

I could not help smiling wryly.

I still had no idea why Zhong Yi, Fan Sicong and Chen Ailing laid the trap for me. What I did know was that it was my stupidity that had helped them learn much about it. They would otherwise have had no idea about it.

It would be meaningless if I went now for Zhong Yi and killed her.

"Hey, buddy, turn around," I told the driver with a sigh.

Chapter IX On the Way to Death

I told the driver I needed to take a piss, and he pulled off the road.

With my bag on my back, I stepped in front of the car and pissed against the reeds before I pulled out my knife.

I turned the handle of the knife as I walked back to the car. The knife reflected the headlights and I heard the noise from the engine growing louder. Immediately I moved to one side of the road before the car rushed over.

The driver made a U-turn in the distance and headed again towards Luntai. He flashed his high-beams, honked three times, rolled the window down, and hurled a torrent of abuse in the wind. He must be pleased with the money instead of a robbery.

I smiled. I was not far from the cabin, and I did not want him to know where I stayed.

Taking off the disguise I had been wearing, I started my second night journey.

Fan Sicong and Chen Ailing would tell me the next morning that Zhong Yi had been on her way back home. They must have invented quite a number of excuses to reassure me, so that I would be willing to finish the journey.

Zhong Yi had sensed the real danger if she stayed with me. She had thought I would kill her and leave at night, but now she realized she had been wrong. I knew well what their new plan was—it was not hard for me to have an educated guess.

I was approaching the house, in front of which was a man.

He was squatting on the ground, his head down and his palms catching the light.

I stepped carefully, but he was too self-absorbed to look up.

I tapped on the vehicle.

"I remember we have bread in the car. I'm hungry."

Yuan Ye was taken aback, but he pocketed his cell phone, ran to me and stepped into the car, when he recognized me.

"Hi," I greeted him. He turned to look at me, his lips curved involuntarily.

"Done?"

"Yeah," he answered, simpering at me in spite of himself.

"Bread," I was trying to remind him.

"Yes, yes." He climbed into the back seat and came out with a packet of croissant.

"Mr. Na, did you come on foot?"

"I had to. It was about half an hour's walk. I couldn't sleep because of hunger. Why are you here outside?" I took the food.

"I was sending text messages. A telephone call had made Fan toss quite a long time in bed. He has just fallen asleep, but I might disturb him with the light from my phone."

"You might have a sleepless night."

Yuan Ye laughed. "We'll chat for a few more minutes and I'll go to bed. You know I have to drive tomorrow."

"You're happy?"

"Yes, I'm even happier than I was when we fell in love. She's really nice to me now, and I'm touched by every word she says to me. She told me she wanted to be my wife."

"Then I helped." I smiled, tearing off a chunk of bread and handing it over. "This is for you."

"I am really hungry." He took it a large mouthful of it. His phone vibrated, apparently with a new message. Ignoring me, he checked it as fast as he could. With the light from the screen, I could see his face was glowing with deep happiness.

"Thinking about your future happy life together with her?"

With a mouthful of bread, he mumbled while busy texting.

I drew my knife and stabbed at him. It went into him between his fourth and fifth rib and pierced his heart. He opened his mouth to scream, but could only stare at me in silence because of the bread. All his hopes and expectations had come to nothing when he was attacked.

He collapsed as soon as my knife penetrated him. I kept the weapon inside him to avoid the blood spurting from the gash. I dragged him away to the sand six to seven meters away from the road. Squatting down, I covered his mouth and nose with my hands. I removed them only several minutes after his body shuddered slightly for the last time, to make sure he would never run away with my knife in his car, while I was dealing with Fan Sicong.

Well, I killed again, twelve years later.

It was an easy job for a cold-blooded murderer. Yes, I was "cold-blooded," and it was the word I used in my books.

And, I had had many books published, and each of them was a rehearsal. I had been so well prepared, both psychologically and technically, that I knew better than ever about death.

I put it into practice again tonight, beautifully and successfully.

I was not sure who Zhong Yi and the others really were. They may be among the ordinary readers of my books, many of whom believed I had been a murderer. They might be the most enthusiastic of them and all this was designed to confirm their hypothesis. But did they ever guess what would happen to them to blow the cover of a potential killer?

Perhaps they did, but they must have underrated it.

To discover the truth about death, one needed the courage to face his own death.

As for Yuan Ye, he was different from the others. He was not at all on his guard against me the first time I met him. He was innocent, but I had no other choice. If I let him go, the others would die meaningless deaths, won't they? He was in my way.

I smelt the smell of blood, feeling that I was what I had been.

I threw my backpack into the car, wrapped two towels around my hands and went for an alloy cable before I pushed open the unlocked door.

The houses for road maintenance workers were structurally the same, but each had their furniture. The different tables and chairs lay in dark shadow.

I travelled among shadows, silently.

The bedroom door was wide open.

I went toward the bed and bent to look at Fan Sicong.

The moonlight filtering through a gap between the curtains fell in a pool on his bottom. I knew it was him, as my eyes adapted to the dim light in the room.

He was lying on his stomach, a position many insecure people preferred because they felt more secure with their chest firmly against the bed.

His head tilted aside, his lips were slightly apart, and he was not snoring.

Putting my hand beside his head, I pressed the mattress so that the space between his head and the bed was wide enough for my cable to go through. It seemed it was not a sound sleep and I saw his eyelids blinking. But it was too late for him—I twisted the cable with my hands and put my weight on him with my knee against his back.

He woke up, twisted his waist frantically and kicked violently, a low gurgle coming out from his throat, like a fish blowing bubbles. He struggled in vain. He tried to get hold of the cable around his neck, but it was so thin that it had gone into his flesh. Frustrated with his fruitless effort to remove the cable, he managed to push me away. Under my weight, he found it hard to turn over, which left him in an awkward position to react. Gradually, he became powerless, and the only thing he could do was to pat on me.

I counted silently. One hundred and seven, one hundred and eight. He was struggling less. Two hundred and seventy-three, two hundred and seventy-four. He was finally motionless. Three hundred and ninety-nine, four hundred. I thought he was dead. I had expected to count to one thousand, a suitably round figure, but I was so bored that I let him go at six hundred and thirty.

Fan Sicong had no idea who killed him. It is said that a dying person can feel like they are floating in the air or see heaven in the last moment of his life. It's also reported that he will experience urinary incontinent. I guessed Fan Sicong must have seen that I was the murderer in the very last minute before his death.

He did not pee too much, but the sheet was all wet. Thank God he did not take a shit.

After I dragged him out of the bed, I took the sheet out to the yard to make it clean. I drew up a bucket of water from a deep well, rubbed the sheet with a soap cake, dried it by squeezing, and hung it up. Zhong Yi had paid for the room, but I left a one-hundred note on the table as an extra, so that the owner of the house would keep silent about the staining of the bed sheet. It was dry and windy, and the sheet would be dry the next afternoon for use at night.

I collected the personal belongings of the two dead people and threw them into my car, before I dragged Fan Sicong's body into the trunk.

I went to Yuan Ye, and dragged him into the desert for about a hundred meters, before I pulled the knife out and turned him over so that his blood would soak into the sand.

He held his phone tight in his hand, and I pried it from his fingers. He had an unread message, and I hit on it while going back.

"💔 Asleep? Wake up and talk to me! 👄 👄"

I flung the phone on the passenger seat, switched on the ignition and headed for Chen Ailing's house.

I will be busy tonight.

For years I had been preparing for the day when it was made clear that I was a killer, by an unusual detective, an idler who did not like me, or even someone who was reborn (I meant her, of course; I had been wondering if she was dead). Sometimes, I couldn't even wait to see what would happen, especially when the fingers of the many gloves fluttered in the breeze, which aroused me sexually.

No one knew that I had rehearsed for it in my book, and my plan in the next one was to let the murderer live to the very end.

For that purpose, I had kept some tools in my bag, to develop my ability to react.

But life would never allow you the time to get ready, and things don't happen as you expect. I had been at a loss when I thought it all out in the Volkswagen, but I had to make a decision as I had no other way out.

It was not a hard decision to make. I knew I would have to take a U-turn soon. If one guy knew that I had killed two people, what I should do was to add one to the number of the dead and to reduce one from that of the people in the know. If more people knew it, I would have to try to do more complicated adding and subtracting. My target would be the person who was stationary and off guard. As for Zhong Yi, I had my own way to deal with her, but I would have to wait until I finished my first phase. So far, things were going well.

I parked my car fifty meters away.

I fastened my knife at my back and held the wire in one hand and the cable in the other. I did not have the towels with me, without which it would hurt my hands when I twisted the cable around the neck. But they were often a burden, and it felt bad with my gloves on. It was rather strange now that I did not feel the discomfort that I had when I was bare-handed.

I put the wire into the keyhole, a slow process which I found myself enjoying. The tension and excitement which had been built up in the two murders began to die down in the delicate work of unlocking the door. My hands were more stable, and it felt as if I could see the inside of the lock when the wire worked against the bolt. The whole world was now under my control again.

It suddenly came to me—or I finally had to admit—that I had my gloves on for years only because I wanted to break with what had been, rather than because I had a fetish about cleanliness. I had been pretending that I was a good guy, I was a novelist, and I had never killed. Without my gloves on my hands, I had to face the world before my eyes, or what I really was.

I was what I had been again, the person who killed.

I laughed quietly.

It was unlocked.

Carefully, I pushed the door.

Clang!

The unexpected noise took me aback. What followed was another clang, but longer. It was the clang of metal, but what metal could make such a horrific sound on the floor?

The door opened. I saw it was a bell on the floor.

It was designed as an alarm, which would fall down to make a noise when the door was pushed open.

I stepped back immediately, but instantly I realized there was no turning back.

So I rushed in.

The inside door was open, but there was no light. I was grateful that I had reacted quickly enough. A few seconds would have allowed Chen Ailing to shut the door close.

I dashed into the room. My feet slipped and I fell down onto the ground.

At the entrance on the floor were all small balls.

Lying on my back, I felt as if I was coming apart. It made me really mad that the old bag was playing these stupid games with me.

An idea flashed across my mind: she had been mad!

I was so badly hurt that I was not able to stand up, but Chen

Ailing, in her nightdress, lunged at me, with a club in one hand and a knife in the other.

What a monster the old bag was!

Her baseball bat was directed at my head, but I parried the blow with my arm. It would have been a much nastier one if she used both of her hands. My arm hurt me badly, but it was tolerable. I reached out to snatch the bat with the other hand, but I got a knife wound in it, which was followed by the second and the third attacks.

I attacked her legs with my own, and she staggered but regained balance with the help of her arms. I drew my knife from my back and stabbed her in the chest when she bent down for the fourth attack at me.

She remained standing with the help of knife, but collapsed beside me when I let her go.

I had no idea if she was dead already, so I rolled away to keep a safe distance from her. With a blow and two knife wounds on my left arm and another knife injury on the shoulder, I began to feel the pain.

I lay still, gasping for breath, but Chen Ailing remained motionless. I managed to rise to my feet and turned on the light, but when I turned back I saw her sitting against the wall, staring at me with her wide eyes.

I lowered myself for the baseball bat.

"A baseball bat is for both hands of yours," I told her. "And you use a knife to stab, not to cut."

She was panting raggedly, mouth open, as if she would die anytime.

"You're tougher than the other two men," I said, holding the bat in my hand, ready for the last, single attack if she struggled to rise to her feet.

What I had said left her clearly disappointed, and the strength she had been gathered to kill me ebbed away instantly.

"They are dead?" she asked.

"Yes, in my car."

"What about Zhong Yi?"

"She'll die in a couple of days—she's not as lucky."

The corners of her mouth turned up and her face contorted. I didn't know whether she was smiling or crying. Perhaps it was because her chest hurt and it was hard for her to breathe.

"It's not my fault, and I have been forced." I moved my chair so that I was opposite her. Blood was oozing slowly from the three wounds I had gotten, but they were only flesh wounds. What an unprofessional attacker she was!

"Well, I'm a writer, but you came to blow my cover when I was in the dark. The problem is you know nothing about what I did, right? You're dying, so tell me about it before you die as a wise woman."

Chen Ailing lowered her head to look at the knife in her chest and then raised it to look at me. Vehicles were rarely heard on the highway across the desert at night, so she must know how helpless she was now.

She started to struggle. Her hands and feet moved frantically to rise, but she was too weak. I remained in my chair and looked at her, and she was almost ready to do it with the help of her bent legs and her hands on the floor when she felt short of breath. She was not noisy, but it was a brutal physical torture. What followed was a coughing fit.

When her fit was over she collapsed, sitting where she had been, but with a different posture.

"Cigarette," she said, between gasps of breath. "In the bag on the head of the bed."

I took the packet and threw it at her.

She pulled out a cigarette with her trembling hands and placed it into her mouth. I watched her flicking her lighter again and again, but it wouldn't catch. I didn't help.

Finally, she succeeded.

"You would cough to death," I said.

She took a long puff at her cigarette, leaving it glowing for quite a while, and then blew the smoke while coughing. I was curious that with only a couple of coughs she looked more energetic and spoke in a louder voice.

"Sir, can you promise me something?"

I shook my head. "I won't let Zhong Yi off. You won't die for nothing, will you?"

"That's not what it is. It will do you no harm, but it will help me die a better death."

"Well, why don't you tell me about your background?"

"I'm a psychologist. I do criminal psychology. Xiao Fan and Zhong Yi were my students."

"What's your research area? The possibility of a mystery writer committing a crime?"

"I study criminal impulses and contexts of crimes. Everyone has the will to commit a crime in a certain context."

"Now you are familiar with the feeling." I knocked the floor lightly with the club.

"It was Zhong Yi who suggested it. She told me you were not a simple guy and was highly sensitive to criminals' moods. We all agree with her, but we've never thought you ever killed. Yes, never. We discussed what case it would be if you killed and you wrote the books, but from the bottom of our hearts, at the subconscious level, Zhong Yi, Fan Sicong, and I have never considered you a murderer. So we had no ready way to deal with it."

Another fit of cough attacked her, and I noticed there was blood in the saliva at the corner of her mouth. I flashed a smile at her.

"Our plan was … Zhong Yi talks with you as a psycho, and with the stories from your computer, we think she can do it well. What she gets from you, your analyses of the case and your ideas of yourself were useful to our study. Actually, the three of us, especially Zhong Yi and me, were your fans. Of course, she was the most enthusiastic one. She believed that you were a person who didn't care when you were cheated. We discussed what would happen … and that's all."

She seemed tired after she uttered these broken sentences. She finished the better part of her cigarette, and I went over to light a new one for her.

"With the help of a friend of mine in the local police bureau, Zhong Yi examined the documentation on four unsolved murder cases in the last five years. They happened in the years of your memory loss, and they are similar to your stories. Our logic was that your crimes should be among those types if you ever killed, and if you didn't, you must know the cases in the stories well, which would help us with our work. Zhong Yi wrote the fragments of the four stories in your style, and Fan Sicong ... he knew well how computers work. It was him who hacked your computer. We started the journey, and things went well. Zhong Yi had her first conversation with you, but she slept with you, which came as a bitter blow to Fan Sicong. After each of your talks, we got together for a discussion, however late it was. Fan Sicong began to resent you, saying you must be a killer."

"He's right," I said.

"I got slightly suspicious of you after your second conversation, because it seemed you were somewhat different. And I guessed Zhong Yi had held something back from us. Anyway, you were right when saying there must be someone who took revenge. What happened in the village was not on our schedule. It was Fan Sicong's idea, and he said the trip should be ended as early as possible because it would become more dangerous if we continue it with a murderer. We had prepared for it by visiting the village earlier. We knew the story about the haunted house, and he suggested our performance in it, for you to tell the truth, and then we report it to the police."

It seemed that I had been quite successful. Fan Sicong's feelings of jealousy of me had misled me, which, in turn, had led to a dramatic change in what would happen.

She finished her second cigarette and had a coughing fit. I offered to light another for her, but she refused.

"If I smoke more, I will die of coughing before I finish. Now that you know what happened, can you do me a favor?"

After a moment of silence, I said, "So, this time, a study?"

She opened her mouth to speak, but she collapsed into another coughing fit.

"Innocent … no … I mean meaningless. Well, you've been curious who I killed?"

"I don't care about it anymore. For years I follow my own habit wherever I spend the night—a bell, balls, and a knife and a club by my bedside. It was a shadow of my childhood. My parents were murdered when I was nine, but it has remained an unsolved case. I was the first to be on the scene, and I see it every time I close my eyes at night. I began to study criminal psychology, want to make it clear why my parents were killed and who did it."

It turned out that she looked better after she finished.

"That's why you smoke when you visit the scene of a crime?"

"You got it. When you talk about the details of a murder and the psychology of a criminal, I find myself visiting the scene of the crime and I feel like smoking. I've been wondering … the case would have been solved if you were me."

"I see what you mean."

I glanced at my watch and it said 3:13 in the morning.

"I guess you're stalling for time, but I don't care. In many stories a person who does so is punished, but I don't set this tired plot in any of my books. Your injury is nasty, and you're dying."

She stared at me in silence.

"You've got at most half an hour," I said. "You must have a list of suspects. I'll have a guess. You're going to meet your parents, and ask them if I'm right."

"They must have already been reborn," she said to herself.

Then she summoned up all her strength to tell her story in the last half hour of her life.

"It was the summer of 1969, in the afternoon of July 13. Cicadas were shrilling. I played outside and went back home at about five. I knocked on the door, but no one answered it. I waited for a quarter of an hour before I went to the backyard. I climbed up a pipe. Our flat was on the first floor, and it was not hard for me. A window was open and I got in through it. I fell on a pool of blood. My mother didn't respond to my calling, so I turned her over. She lost her face. The lamp was beside her, and its iron base was covered with what was on her face. I went for my father, crying. He was in an armchair in his study, with his head drooping. He was covered with blood, and the wall before him was covered with blood, too. I rushed over to shake him. I held his head up, and I saw his eyes were wide open with anger. He had a bad cut across his neck. It was the only injury to his body, but I saw no murder weapon. I was frightened to death, but I overturned the cups, two of them, on the tea table when I ran away. I fell down on the ground and fainted. It was dark when I recovered. I started to cry and a neighbor heard me and knocked at the door. It was Uncle Li living downstairs. He broke in and called the police. He tried to carry me away, but I held my father's leg. The policemen came, an old man and two younger men, and I ..."

Chen Ailing paused for a breath. That was the way she spoke and she never finished a long sentence without stopping in the middle.

"I ..." She paused again.

And then she repeated the same word, "I ..."

She looked straight ahead as she spoke, but gradually she lost her focus and her pupils were dilated. She looked up at me, meaningfully. Then her eyelids lowered before her eyes closed.

I went over and put my hand before her nose. She was not breathing.

It took her six minutes.

I returned to my chair.

"Two people," I said.

"You father must know one of them. They talked in the study instead of the meeting room, so what they discussed must be private affairs. His eyes were wide open means he was badly shocked at what was happening to him, which means they were probably very familiar with each other. You said no weapon had been available at the scene, and I sensed from the tone of your voice that it should not be one of your kitchen knives. Of course, a study is not a place for knives. So the visitor came with the knife, and the attempt on your father's life was a designed one. He was so skillful that he did it with a single slash through his throat. But the guy who killed your mother was much more impetuous, both psychologically and technically. It could be a woman novice, who may be the wife of the other guy. So the wives must be chatting causally in a different room, while their husbands were in the study, talking. The task for the woman should be to distract your mother's attention away from what the husbands were doing. But noises came from the study. Your mother was about to see what was happening when she was hit on the head with a lamp post, something within the reach of the frantic wife.

"You talked about the study in your house. That means you had at least three rooms—a study, a sitting room, and a bedroom, and you owned an iron standard lamp. At that time, it was a house only for a high-ranking official, a well-known show business personality, or a capitalist, which I guess was your father. 1969 was the third year of the Cultural Revolution period, and the whole country was absolutely chaotic. It was the once-in-a-lifetime chance for the nationalist Kuomintang to defeat the Communists on the mainland. Your family status and how your parents were murdered point to the conclusion that the murders had to do with the shadowy world of espionage between the two sides. Well, I have to stop now—you know, I have to finish in six minutes."

I opened the medical case in my car for a bandage, which I twisted around my injured limb. Then I began to clean up the room. It was not as easy as the previous one because of the blood—much of it was mine. Luckily, the bed was stained. There were a few drops on the wall, but I removed them with water.

I mopped the floor a couple times until no traces of blood were visible. I had dumped Yuan Ye's body in the desert for his blood to flow, so that the bag would not be stained. I had thought I could do the same with Chen Ailing, but now it seemed I did not have the time. After I managed to get Fan Sicong into the back of my car, I spread the old newspapers from the house on the trunk and wrapped Chen Ailing's clothes around her own chest, before I placed her into it, her face upwards and her legs curling up.

With everything done, I returned to the house to collect up Chen Ailing's private belongings. I was on my knees searching for any missing balls when her telephone started to ring.

It was Zhong Yi calling.

I answered it.

"Hi Mrs. Chen! I'm now at the airport in Korla, and the earliest flight is due in more than three hours. Sorry to wake you up, but he texted me. I replied to him but got no answer. I called him but his phone shut down. So I was afraid …"

I sighed.

It immediately silenced her.

"So you take the earliest flight to Urumqi for another one to Kashgar, to collect evidence in Khan Palace about my crime? How can you be so sure you will find the body when we're at Kashgar in four days so I can be arrested by the police?"

"Where's Teacher Chen?"

"You're so nervous and your voice has changed."

"Where's Teacher Chen?"

"She's with Fan Sicong and Yuan Ye."

After a moment of silence, she started to scream.

"Shush. You're a clever woman, so be quiet. It's a public place, but it doesn't matter much as there must be few passengers around you at this time of the day."

"I'll call the police. You're dead!"

"Don't do that. You've got to calm down before we continue. You know me well, and I have good reasons to answer your call and to tell you not to report to the police. You'll regret it if you do it."

I heard she was asked what was wrong. After a moment of silence, she said something, which I failed to catch, before she moved to a different place.

"Go ahead."

"For years, I've been preparing for it: money, false ID, and new identity. I've been happy about my identity as a writer, but I can change into a different one when necessary, perfectly and immediately. If you report me to the police, I will vanish in a minute. But I've told you I like my identity as a writer. Because it brings some trouble when the police know it, I'll vow to take my revenge on you by killing you. I will do it next month, next year or in ten years—I'll do it whenever I want. You'll have to be on your guard all the time, but to err is human. Don't you think so?

"Now I have something for you and me—a game. You go ahead with your plan in Kashgar, but you have four days to look for the crime scene and the body. You find them and call the police, and I lose the game. I'll then find a good place for myself and never come to trouble you, allowing you a peaceful life. But when you fail to find them when I come, I'll make sure you're dead. When you're killed, it will be impossible for the police to know how the group of us has vanished from the earth. The problem is you will be the number one suspect, because I can change my identity easily. I can even find ways to keep my writer identity. You see, this is a fair game and both of us have our chance to win it. The rules of the game: first, don't even think about reporting me to the police. Believe it or not, I'll know it and escape when you do it. Second, don't leave any message for anyone. You might expect it helps in avenging your death when you lose, but you know you'll leave your family behind.

"Well, what's that noise? Are your teeth chattering? Sorry, what a mess we have made! Believe me, I didn't mean it. But when it comes to us, we can only choose to face it. Am I right?"

"Yes, I think you're right," said the other voice. "The problem is I know too little about it. It's not a fair game. I bet my life on it, but you can leave whenever you want. Tell me the exact time."

I smiled, and I could feel the adrenaline flooding my body.

"July 18, 1999," I answered.

"A hint about the location?"

"You're asking too much. You didn't know much about the location and the time, but you went to Kashgar. I like you, and it is the place where the road branches off. Hope you can win. I mean it."

Chapter X In Kashgar

As usual, we were a team of four, but I was the driver tonight. When I was ready to carry Yuan Ye back, he was not bleeding anymore and the sand on which he lay was stained red. Blood dried quickly in the dry and windy desert, and in no time the stained grains were either swept away or covered up by new sand, leaving no traces of what had happened.

Realizing there was no time to lose, I drove like the clappers. At ten to five, when Tazhong was already seventy kilometers behind us, I slowed down to turn off the highway.

It was a great car, and it didn't get stuck in the sand. I drove off into the desert for about half an hour before I came to a stop in front of a sand dune. I was about thirty kilometers from the road. I buried the three bodies, together with the entire luggage, in a pit I dug with a shovel from my car. It looked as if a stiff wind was on its way, which would move the dune to where I stood. In a few hours the bodies would be under sand several meters or even more than ten meters. In this unsettled area, they could be there for a century without being discovered.

I backtracked to the highway at six thirty, when it was still dark. There was not a single soul on the road. The wind began blowing and it was blurring my tracks.

I had my breakfast at Mingfeng before I walked two blocks

to my inn.

When I woke up after a restful sleep, the sun was already high in the sky. I headed to the parking lot, and from a distance I could see it was not there. I had left the key in the ignition and the window half-open. As I had expected, the guy who had stolen it understood me accurately. I didn't think I had left any trace in the car other than some hairs and skin scrapings. And I was sure it would be repainted soon and a new license plate would be seen on it.

Text messages kept coming in for Yuan Ye. I read a couple of them and answered for him. The sender seemed quite relieved and became more passionate. I did it again every several hours, making believe that I was driving and could only text during breaks. It had been ages since I last whispered sweet nothings in an ear and I felt rather embarrassed to do it, which was prefect in misleading the police. But I knew that I meant more. I was a great actor in the two days in which the weird relationship lasted, because I knew what had happened. For several times, I felt a sudden impulse to end it with impolite language, but I gave up. The night when I was at Hetian, she called again and again and the phone rang for more than five minutes, as if she would keep doing it unless it was answered. As I had been using it for nearly sixty hours, the old phone beeped a couple of times to indicate low battery while it was ringing, before the screen darkened. I took out the SIM card and snapped it into two, removed the battery, and smashed the phone into pieces before dumping in the dustbin.

Goodbye must be waved after such a long trip, as the Chinese saying goes.

I travelled all the way west, in a stranger's car or in a bus, purely by intuition. It was an easy journey at the beginning and I took my time in doing everything. As I was approaching Kashgar, I became more restless. It was not because I feared that I would lose the game. It would be narrow defeat even if I did. It is said that one becomes restless when he is coming back home from afar. Kashgar is not my hometown, but it was the place where I was reborn. My memory of my teenage years had faded into nothing, but a devil had been born out of blood. In the previous twelve years, I had never returned to Kashgar, my Achilles' heel, which was a weakness that I had to overcome.

Then I sped up.

It was by noon three days after the killings that I arrived at Kashgar, a day earlier than I had promised Zhong Yi.

It seemed that Kizil River had become my critical line. My heart began to beat irregularly immediately after I crossed it. It skipped a beat from time to time, showing a wide crack, from which those memories of the past came flooding back. Just as what happened on a freshly ploughed field, I saw numerous worms, black or red, with or without shells, and large or small.

I got across the river on a creaky cart with an old man, who guided me into that house on the stage. He pointed to a room, and I could see a path that branched off.

The memories kept flooding back and linked with one another. They had always been there in my mind, but they had never revived. What I had recalled again and again was simply the scenario how I waved a knife in a place with flashing light and how blood splashed in rhythm with my moments. Memories are like a knife. They cut out narrow paths, which criss-cross to form a labyrinth.

That was the only vague part in my memory of those five years. It was vague not because something was missing, but because it was so impressive that I had a feeling as if I was in dream. Now I had no idea what I had had in mind when I thought about it as I left Kashgar after the shock. I had written many stories, which all had their inspirations from the pool of blood. As it was repeated, it had expanded steadily until it was three times of the original size. I felt as if the many of me were murdering at the same time, but each of me was doing it in a slightly different manner—chopping, slashing, torturing.

As I was approaching Khan Palace, my memories of what

had happened twelve years ago flooded back. They were not only images—the smell filled the air around me. But I saw no images of her. I knew she was there in my memory, but I saw no images of her. I was sitting next to the old man on a flatcar and his feet were against my waist, but where was she? He pointed to the door on which the carvings were covered with dust and told me it was my room, but where was she? I remembered she had been with us, but where had she been? How weird! I could not help but recall what had happened that day with her.

"You're a goddess but you're profaned, and let me see if you're white and pure inside," I told her after I had killed the old man. Then I held up my knife to her, but did I bring down it with a thud?

Or did I stop in the middle. Did I let her go?

"Here you go again! Here you go again! This is a matter of life and death for her, for which I've always at a loss," I said to myself. "If she's still alive, why hasn't she come to me? Leave her alone! What I have to do now is to deal with Zhong Yi."

In the distance was the raised platform.

I got seated in a restaurant and began to dial. I was calling a friend of the driver who took me to Kashgar, a gangster who lived at Khan Palace. He made a living by selling artificial jade, but he killed much of his time either fooling around or gambling.

When the beautifully prepared dishes were served, the guy came in with a big smile on his face, although it was the first time we met. I told him I came from Korla and was here to look for a job as a tour guide. I preferred a job at the palace, and I needed someone who was familiar with this place to help me.

When we were all feeling a bit tipsy, I asked him about what was happening in the region. He rambled, but I clearly sensed that there was nothing that had aroused suspicion by the local police around Khan Palace. Kashgar had been a region with sensitive ethical issues, and a police's presence could be easily noticed and even officers in plain clothes could be immediately recognized.

Zhong Yi had not reported me to the police, which was only to be expected. After I told him what she looked like, he asked jokingly if she was my woman. I told him that she was hesitating about my proposal. He was drunk and said without thinking that she had been around for a couple of days.

"A gorgeous woman!" He wrapped my shoulders with his arms and I could smell liquor on his breath. "A total babe. Come on … bring her with you next time for a drink."

When asked more about her, he said nothing but babbled to urge me to drink more, as if he would collapse anytime.

I didn't think I could learn anymore from him. A ticket was needed to enter the palace. It was most probable that the palace people would have noticed when a woman as pretty as Zhong Yi came and left. They even might remember how she came and left.

She must have left some traces of her presence during her process of investigation. The more work she did, the more traces she left. So it was not extremely hard for me to figure out where she was.

The guy buried his face in his arms at the table, unable to help me anymore. I rose, ready to pay the bill, when he looked up and held my arm in his hands. "Yes, you go for her and bring her here."

I patted his hand, ready to persuade him to relax his grip on me, but his face creased into an encouraging smile, "I know where she stays."

Twenty minutes later, I was standing before her house.

It was neither an inn nor a hotel, but an ordinary house commonly seen at Khan Palace in Kashgar. For two days Zhong Yi stayed there. She was clever enough not to stay in a hotel or an inn, which would request her personal identification that I could manage to obtain. She expected to keep her name secret by choosing a room in a private house, but that would make no difference to me.

The Khan Palace perched high on a cliff. Built by Uighurs

more than a thousand years ago, it was nothing different from the well-known dwellings for common residents on the opposite cliff. The Khan Kingdom in Kashgar in the 9th century was a small state and the palace, rather simple in design, is dramatically different from similar structures in central China. Traditionally, the local houses were built according to features of a terrain, so was the palace, part of which was underground. The whole building had been destroyed and rebuilt, but the underground part had completely collapsed and it was impossible to enter it. Inside it must be a huge honeycomb-shaped structure, like an underground labyrinth, which was full of secrets.

The house in which Zhong Yi stayed was along the western edge of the cliff. It was a three or four-storied construction, and the top level had an entrance high on the cliff and the door to the ground level faced the road under the cliff.

The door was closed. I looked up at the house for a while for its exact location and then climbed up a winding path nearby leading to the top level. Tickets were required to enter the palace, but the local Uighur people knew how to get there through other paths unknown to outsiders.

The cliff was full of intersecting paths only about two meters wide. Strangers often found themselves in a dead end after several turns.

"You've got to look at the tiles on the ground—the oblong ones mean you're going to a dead end, and you have to follow the ones with six angles," the old man told me twelve years ago.

I had hinted to Zhong Yi that it was where the path branched off, and I had been careless enough to mention that the bones were somewhere under the palace. If she still remembered what I said, she would be able to link the two. Actually, there was an entrance at the point where the path branched off, which lead into the labyrinth.

But there were many paths that forked here, so my hint to Zhong Yi was not at all helpful to her. It may have been misleading, too. When what was at stake was a choice between life and death, courtesy hardly mattered. It would be foolish of her if she took it seriously.

The place looked almost the same as it had been twelve years ago. The poor still lived in houses with abode walls, and the rich in yards with fig trees and decorations of elaborate brick carvings. The only changes included added levels to their houses and new projections across village lanes. Most gates were wide open for visitors, who were expected more to buy their homemade items than to look around the houses.

I took a turn along the road, and in no time I was before the house where Zhong Yi stayed. The indigo gate stood open. It looked like a two-storied building, but it should be four or five stories tall, considering the height I had reached.

I went into it. The side room was open for business, and a customer was choosing among the jade items. Sitting leisurely cross-legged, the owner of the shop simply ignored me. Without a second thought, I walked to the main room, which had a long splice glass skylight and a spiral staircase leading to the higher level. Sunlight through the skylight fell in a pool on the stairs, along which were two lines of potted plants.

It was quiet and I did not see a soul in sight. The rooms along the rail were knocked through between each other, and in them were several women weaving tapestries. The walls were covered with their finished products, but there were no customers. I went down a flight of stairs, for my experience told me that Zhong Yi must have been arranged to live on the ground or first floor.

I felt strange that vague images of the past seemed to flash into my mind. My heart missed a beat, and I almost missed my footing. I stood on the stairs for quite a long time before I realized what before me was just like what I had seen the old man's house.

I knew the local houses were similar in structure. For example, the staircases in them were one of the few types. But I did feel something unusual about the house.

So I went all the way down to the ground level, without stopping on the first floor.

Yes, it had exactly the same layout.

In the middle of the ground floor was a spacious hall with a skylight as high as more than ten meters above my head. I could also see the square railings around the three upper levels, which were covered with green veins. The straight staircases were along the wall, except the one between the ground and the first floors, which were about the two-thirds of the others in length, leading to the middle of the northern wall and facing the gate. In front it was a large platform with a railing. Four stairs down the platform was the sitting room, making it like a split-level construction.

I went down to the platform, moved on a few paces, and took the stairs down to the sitting-room. On each side of me was a corridor, half of the width of the platform, which led to rooms on the ground floor.

The old man had lived on the ground floor, in a house with a similar layout.

This was where the path branched off!

It was inside the house, instead of outside. There was a forked path every several minutes as a guest walked along the streets around the palace on the cliff. Misled, no one could have possibly thought about that it was inside in a house. It was logical for me to choose a place where I could have a bath and change my clothes before I left, when I was covered with blood after I killed the two guys.

But I had never thought Zhong Yi lived in a similarly structured house. Could she possibly have the same idea? I began to regret telling her about it.

I walked toward the back of the staircase, where I saw a small door. I was not surprised to see it in a house with a similar structure. It was a storeroom. Behind the door of the old man's storeroom was the cover of the secret tunnel, which was under an old blanket and a tool box. What could be seen in this one?

I walked on before stopping before a closed door. "It was the room I rented from the old man twelve years ago. Is it where Zhong Yi lives?" I wondered.

Remarkable coincidences do happen in real life.

Most doors in the building were left open or ajar, so the rented room must be among the closed ones.

It was afternoon, and Zhong Yi must be outside, wondering along the streets to search for the path that branched off. Is it a good idea to stay in the room waiting for her? I thought. It would take me less than a minute to pick the lock.

"Hi!" a voice came from behind me.

Scared, I turned as quickly as I could.

It was a Uighur woman in her fifties, one of three carpet weavers on the second floor.

"Hi!" she greeted me again, smiling.

"Hi!" I responded in Uighur.

"I'm here looking for a friend. She stayed here for a couple of days."

She could hardly suppress her surprise.

I was wondering whether I got it wrong or was in the wrong place.

"Yes, a woman was here, but she's left."

Zhong Yi left today, and she had asked the landlord where she could find a train ticket agency this morning.

I arrived one day earlier, but she left one day earlier.

Escaped? Was she prepared to live in the shadow of death for the rest of her life, without the courage to fight through with me to the end?

No, it wasn't what she would do. She was a woman who was smart and courageous enough.

Why by train instead of by air? Where was she going? Urumqi? If she intended to escape, she would have traveled by air directly to her destination. But it would be impossible for me to know her whereabouts if she left by train. Was it true?

No. No, no, no, no, no.

It was unusual to ask the landlord about the ticket office, as the information is easily available on the Internet or the ticket could be bought at the railway station. Why did a woman who played a game of murder with me show what she was doing so clearly?

It must be a decoy tactic of hers. What she had said was for me, because she knew I would follow her here.

So she was not on a train. Would it be a plane?

I went down the stairs to the labyrinth.

Continuing to act as a man who adored her, I had learned enough about what Zhong Yi had been doing from her landlord. And I was puzzled by two facts: she wandered about for quite a long time at the foot of the staircase on the ground floor, and she asked about the small door under the staircase. She did it last night, and she decided early in the morning to leave one day earlier and she asked about the ticket agency.

She was the toughest opponent of mine.

She didn't leave at all. Thinking that I would come for her, probably earlier than she had expected, she must have decided to gain time by misleading me.

Everything was clear to me. Because she thought stalling for time would be to her advantage, she must be confident about what to do next. It was at this last precious moment of hers, when she was hovering between life and death, that she was bursting with energy and doubled her wisdom. At this time, it would be incredibly foolish of her to count on any of my slips.

If I considered the bottom of the staircase was where the path branched off, what would I I would ask how many houses had been left empty in the past years, because the way to the labyrinth would have been discovered if they were used. How did she enter the houses, through the door or the window? This was her own business. It had been three hours since she left at about half past eleven, leaving me no time to waste. Where were those houses on the cliff which had been left empty? Three or five? What about the houses which had been unoccupied for twelve years? If this was one of her own questions, would she be told that there is only one such house. "Go straight on and then turn left. Turn right when you see a square-shaped stone at the end of alley. It was the one on your right when you pass an overhead projection spanning the lane."

Was she in the labyrinth now?

I walked carefully ahead to the center of the labyrinth. My false beard is soaking wet with sweat, and I could feel its weight. It seemed I was covered with a fine translucent glaze, which could only be removed by soaking it by blood after it was ripped open with the help of a knife.

I was before the square-shaped stone, and I turned right.

The alley was empty of people, but I could see an invisible figure of a man walking ahead as my guide. It was the old man I had met twelve years ago. But she was nowhere to see.

"I wonder if you've got a family." I remember that was what I had said. It was at that very moment that I saw why the old man would leave me alone in a small inn in Kashgar for a couple of days. I was wrong in thinking that he left for a big jade dealer, as he returned to the town only when he got pieces of precious jade.

Treating me as a lucky laborer, he never allowed me to go home with him. I didn't care, and I didn't give a damn. I remembered he had broken one of my ribs, slapped my face so hard that it had left me deaf in one ear for half a month, and touched her with his filthy neck, face, and lips. F--k, it was nothing that he refused to take me home with him.

But why did he bring me back home that year?

Yes, it was the overhead projection spanning the lane. I would see her when I passed it. But I would be earlier, so I would have to wait for her beside the staircase.

It turned cloudy all of a sudden.

What smell?

Before my eyes was a rather open space when I walked through the projection. It was starkly open, contrasting sharply with the surrounding part of the palace. I stopped.

A local man was crossing the turning behind me with a wheelbarrow. Hearing the noise, I walked up toward him.

"What has happened there?"

"What do you mean?" he asked casually while turning his head to the direction in which I pointed, as if the place was nothing special in the town.

"Oh, I see," he said after a moment of confusion. "It burned down years ago."

During an earthquake four years ago, a fire had broken out in a house behind the projection. It had not been contained in time as the neighboring house was vacant. The fire had gutted the building, and the local government had had the charred shell removed, intending to rebuild it. The project had been delayed due to lack of funding, leaving it deserted. At the same time, it had become the de facto dump for the villagers and the stink was so overpowering that it had been avoided as a "no-go area" at the palace.

The overhead projection had been deserted, too. The air was filled with the stench of stale urine as I was under it.

Now, I found myself in the "no-go area."

Focusing on the scene, I felt happy that the old man's house had been ruined. When Zhong Yi asked about empty houses in the village, no one would tell her about this one, because it was no longer a house.

It was an open area, but the pale sky did not look higher. Instead, it lowered itself into a gray blanket. Standing on the heap of rubble, I surveyed the place. On a broken wall were blue mosaic tiles, and a few remaining pieces of gray plaster could be observed between the bricks in the niches beside it.

Slowly and exactly on the spot, I saw a three-storied construction coming out of the ground. It was growing taller and taller, until it was so high that I had to raise my head for it. It moved in the way water waves did, but it was as firm as a gravestone. It seemed it was within my reach.

I moved over to it.

It had all happened about the same time of the day, three to four o'clock in the afternoon, in a quite sunny afternoon. I had been awoken from my dream when I had a short nap after lunch in my dingy room. I still remembered it was a noise that had disturbed me. I pushed the door open and found myself alone in a deadly quiet house. Thinking about the noise, I went to the place where the road branched off. Before me was a small unlocked door. Pulling it open, I saw a rolled-up blanket, a toolbox out of place, and an oblong cover of a secret passage, which had been pushed aside.

Moving one step forward, I was outside the house of my memory and in the meeting room on the ground floor that had been ruined. I saw among the hump of rubble the furniture and vessels. I was greatly surprised that I remembered them so well. Looking around, I felt I was nearly a patient of temporary insanity.

I turned right to a gradual descent. It was higher than the floor, but there should be a platform and stairs under the earth. At a corner were a few cement slabs which leant against a broken wall to from a small space. This was where the storage room had been. A curved door plank stood before the secret passage like its last guard, leaving it half-hidden.

I approached the plank with two long steps, and I was surprised at what was before my eyes.

It was a dark hole!

The cement cover was beside it, but the fresh traces told me it had just been removed.

Well, I was late.

But I was not too late, as Zhong Yi was still inside.

A weak voice inside me told me to put the cover back, but I ignored it. Instead, I climbed down.

I did it with utmost caution, so no noise was made. It was very dry here and powdery dust kept coming into my nose, as if the earth particles from the previous visitor were still flying. The first section was extremely narrow with tiny stairs, just like a hole for grave robbers. It became wider two meters down and the wall was reinforced with long granite blocks.

The underground part of Khan Palace had system of its

own. A basement was built along with a house, and it was either used or deserted when the house was re-built. What had made it more complicated were the many deep holes left by generations of pottery makers and the underground passageways had constructed in the reign of Khan Dynasty. It remained unknown whether the passages had been for treasures or for defense purpose, and its scale had not been documented. Much of the three interlocked structures had collapsed in earthquakes, but in other parts they had been joined up.

The size and the structure of the passage I was now in told me it must have built when the Khan Palace was constructed. It should have been one of the entrances, but it has been covered more than a thousand years later with two meters of earth, which had been removed later when the house above it was rebuilt.

My feet reached the ground. The passage was about two meters high, a fair size in the region, although it was nothing compared with the impressive tombs for emperors in central China. It became lower as I walked forward. I took my torch and knife with me and left my bag behind on the ground. I was now somewhere in the middle of the passage, so I could head for either of the two ends. But I could only choose one of the directions, because the other side was a dead end. I knew it because I had been here twelve years ago.

With my flashlight in my left hand and the knife in the right, I moved slowly forward. I listened hard, but there was nothing special. Zhong Yi might have been far ahead of me or she might be standing in the dark holding her breath. A few steps further, I saw two much narrower branch-off passages of the height of about one and half meters, leading to my left and right sides. The passage I was in must be the main one. I would take neither of the other two, because their roofs had caved in.

I walked forward while trying to recalling the way. I remembered the passage turned westward in front of me. The bulb of a tungsten lamp over my head was still there, but it was disconnected. I moved my torch and it seemed the stones in the rubble became alive. As I had revealed my position, it had given Zhong Yi an advantage if she would attack me now. But I was not worried, because as an untrained murderer, she would not be so vicious as to kill me with one blow.

I knew a few steps ahead was the old man's secret chamber, a room more than fifty meters where his best jade materials were shelved. Twelve years ago, I took a stone from the shelves close to the entrance. It had been the greatest gain for us that year—I had discovered it in the upstream of the river. But now I wore it on my chest.

A twenty-year-old young man, I had embarked on an adventure in the underground passages one afternoon. I had tried every one of them before I found myself in the secret chamber. It had become the old man's private room for his valuables, as there was only one passage left to it. The three generations in my family had been jade dealers and I had seen a vast variety of jade stones, but I had been surprised at what was before my eyes in the room. The dim light from the tungsten lamp and the dozens of candles had not allowed me to see how white they were, but I had been fascinated by their quality. With that suet jade in my hand, I was looking for other small pieces that I could take away with me when a low, unclean but rushing sound was heard from the other end of the room. My view had been blocked by the shelves, and I began to walk to it, holding my breath.

My memory was suddenly interrupted.

Because I found myself in a dead end.

The wide passage caved in, completely. It must be the result of the earthquake a few years ago—both the houses on the ground and the underground passages had been destroyed and what had happened here would be a secret for the coming generations.

This is great and there is nothing left for Zhong Yi, I thought.

But wait. Where is she? She was here earlier and she must be here now. The passage was blocked, but where's she now?

A branch passage, I realized quickly. I had come through the right passage because I knew what it was, but she had to try again and again. She must be in a branch passage now.

I switched off my light and waited for her.

I was about twenty to thirty meters from the entrance, so I could see a little daylight although the passage formed a 45-degree bend before me. As I was in pitch darkness, I would see Zhong Yi when she appeared before she could see me.

The light filtering through the entrance began to dance when I stared at it long enough. I had to blink to focus again, to make sure that it was an illusion and that no other source of light interfered. Zhong Yi would have to have her own flashlight. As the two narrow turn-off passages were short dead ends, it was the time for her to appear, even if she had been down here five minutes earlier than me and she had been slow as a snail.

Everything around was frightfully quiet, aside from my heart beating and breathing and the occasional sound of my stomach's rumbling.

"Where is Zhong Yi?" I wondered.

An idea suddenly popped into my head: would new passages be created, as old ones have been blocked in the earthquake?

Switching on my flashlight, I walked back.

The road branched off, and I took one of the two as I pleased and lowered myself into it.

There was a reinforcement layer of granite inside the main passage. The smaller branch passage I was now in was simply an underground tunnel. It seemed to me that the earth had been rammed down when it was built, but it was much more dangerous after so many years of erosion.

The small passage zigzagged, as if it were built by a boa constrictor. After three turns, I was at the end, which was formed by more rubble than it had been. A marked change was the wall on my left about three meters from the end—it was collapsing from the top. With the help of my flash, I looked into it and saw a large space before me.

The crack was about three meters deep. I managed to go through it, without fearing it would cave in and bury me. If I believe in fate, the guy would be expecting something more than my death half way in the tunnel, I thought.

Snaking my way forward, I could hear rodents ahead of me. As I was reaching the opposite side, I suddenly spotted a fat black rat near my face, which stood motionless in the patch of light from my torch staring at me intently. Thinking that it was the rat king, who came out to see what was happening, I bared my teeth at it and it simply vanished from sight. Immediately, I heard many more rats scurrying noisily around. When I was out, I shone my torch around me, but I saw none of them.

I thought there were quite a number of exits here, at least for rats. And then I realized they were for people, too.

It was a basement, with some rotting tables and old wooden boxes in it. I saw no modern devices such as electronic bulks, so I had no idea how many years ago the basement had been built. Much of the wall had collapsed. Instead of looking around for other furniture, I examined a crumble and saw two cracks leading outside. I took the one beside the old man and found myself in a different passage.

I was not sure if I was following Zhong Yi. She may have chosen a different passage among the many new ones created as a result of the last earthquake, which seemed to have brought about a massive change in this underground world. She may have gone into a different crack, or she may have done it even earlier. I knew well where the old man's body was, and it seemed as if I had been led by a dipper, which was somewhere giving a dim light, toward death. But, in this underground labyrinth, Zhong Yi had to try her luck by guessing in choosing among the many roads.

Afraid that she would have a lucky guess, I would have to be there earlier to wait for her.

As I was already here, I would do more than killing Zhong

Yi. I somewhat missed the old man, and I had the desire to see him. I wanted to see the girl again, too. I wanted to know if she had become a skeleton, just as the old man had. She was dead, but I wanted to confirm it. Now I was so close to her—she was simply about one hundred meters away from me as the crow flew, but in my mind her image was so unclear that it seemed to be wrapped in a veil of mist. Was I wildly excited?

I was destined to face what I had been twelve years before since the day I returned to Kashgar. I must admit that I had been changed by what had happened to me after I passed though the treasure house and what I had done in response. I had changed so much that I had to live with it in the past years, reviewing it again and again. My memory of it began to be twisted, leaving me unsure about whether it was me who killed her.

I needed a thorough cleaning, before I became a different person.

I was approaching her.

I was approaching her after I walked through three walls in the way a magician did, but I outflanked before I closed in again. Another half hour later, I was sure I was just a footstep away; probably she was on the other side of the wall. But I found myself in a dead end.

I started to get frustrated, wondering if I had to go back. I tried several forked roads and cracks which I had ignored, but realized none of them would possibly lead to the direction of my destination.

Then I caught a sudden flash of light.

Was it an illusion?

I switched off my torch.

I saw a flash of light, but it was not from my torch.

I waited quietly for a few second before the light flashed again. It was from the wall on my right.

There was a crack running up the wall, which was so thin that my finger could not reach into it.

With my eyes on the crack, I backed away slowly until my

back was against the wall behind me. Then I sprint with all my strength.

This is my last ditch attempt, I thought before I banged the wall with my shoulder. The wall collapsed, and I hurt my shoulder, but not as badly as I had done in the cellar. I rolled over and, when I looked up, a beam of harsh light shone on my face. I could see the figure of Zhong Yi in the dark background, but I couldn't read the expression on her face. My torch was nowhere to find, but I was lucky enough that I held the drawn knife in a firm grip. With the help of left hand on the floor, I made a sudden dive for her chest with the weapon.

I stabbed at her.

As deep into her as I could.

Kneeling on one knee before her, I felt something warm on my face. It was a drop of blood of hers.

The torch clattered to the floor, but she cut at me with the knife she firmly held in her other hand. She was rather slow because of the pain in her body. Moving my head to one side, I hit her wrist with my fist, and she lost her grip of the knife.

As she was stepping backward with an anguished cry, I pulled my knife out of her. She had been stabbed in the midriff, a less vital area, and another thrust was needed to kill her.

She retreated two more steps before falling down on the ground, but I was already on my feet. I stepped before her in one long step. The torch on the ground pointed at me. I kicked it hard and it was rotated 180 degrees, lighting up her and the desiccated corpse beside her.

She was lucky that it was the right place for her. But I was lucky, too.

Pressing her stomach with her hands, she saw the omen of death, her face paled with fright.

That was her moment of death. I had much to say to her, but I gave up. It was useless and funny for someone who would kill her to speak to her. Holding the knife tighter, I lowered my shoulders and humped myself.

"Wait!" she cried.

"I've got it," her voice trembled. "I won the game."

"You were far too slow."

"But you were one day earlier," she shouted again.

I could not help laughing, "So I have to say sorry to you? I'm sorry. Okay?"

"Wait a moment. Only one person was dead here. You see, one corpse only."

Suddenly my heart seemed to turn to ice, as if something inside me was about to collapse, so I had to be physically restrained. I put my toes at the end of the torch and slowly I rotated it on the ground. The fan-shaped light swept the room.

I saw the shelves, shelves that once stood like towers, with jade statues on their tops. But the pieces of art now lay all over the floor like dead bodies, their heads scattered between them.

The folding chair was at the far end of the house. The man must have enjoyed his moments when he curled up in the chair and the towers—his own treasure—were before his appreciating eyes. If the tungsten filament lamps were not bright, the candles on the towers could be used, which would give a ghostly glow to the house.

Zhong Yi was beside the chair. She was examining the man in the chair when she was attacked. The old man reclined on the seat. He had not been reduced to a skeleton, as I had expected, but a mummy. But I was not surprised, as it was extremely dry here.

I didn't fix my eyes on the dark naked body for too long before I continued to search with the help of my flashlight. I then saw a collapsed mud wall, a crack through which an adult could pass, and my own feet.

I scanned the whole of the place. Zhong Yi was right that it was the only one body in the house.

"I have been wrong in thinking you killed two guys, the old man and his daughter. There's only one body, so the daughter was not murdered here. You're right. She is not dead, she escaped, and sooner or later she will come back for you."

I was pretty sure what she needed was more time, which would be her one last hope to cling to. She had to mess with my mind until she could get a fighting chanceBut there was only one f--king body here!

I felt almost dazed, feeling emotions bubbling up inside me. I struggled to force them back, but in vain. They were so forceful that I found my head ready to crack.

I could do nothing but stood around. Don't stand there all dazzled—kill the guy in front of you before it is too late, said a voice inside my head. But the struggle with the emotions had left me utterly exhausted. Who knew what would have happened if I had failed in bottling them up.

I eventually noticed what Zhong Yi was doing. One of her hands snaked its way to a knife, the knife on the ground.

All of a sudden, all that I had in my mind disappeared and I shouted at her, "Go to the hell!"

I held my knife high in the air, and she began to scream, tears coming to her eyes.

It comforted me greatly. I slashed her with the knife, but she rolled away. I missed because I did it slowly on purpose, so that I could see how the pretty, wise, and determined woman struggled for life at the moment of death.

I kicked her on the bottom.

"You move again? Getting the knife? Can you do it again?"

"No, no, no. I didn't pick it up ... it's not mine."

She was already incoherent with fear. With a brittle laugh, I kicked on the torch to point it at her before I hold up my knife.

"Wait, wait. At the moment of death can you tell me what happened years ago? It was weird, wasn't it? If she escaped by feigning death, why she didn't call the cops? Why didn't the neighbors notice?"

She struggled to be calm, but she was shivering with fear and tears came down her cheeks. How ridiculous she was!

But what she said upset me—she tried to catch me on the raw.

She survived, but why didn't she come and take her revenge? She survived, but why didn't she come and take her revenge? Was she alive?

She had to be dead immediately.

"I'll look for the answers when you are dead."

"You're not a merciless killer, are you?"

It was funny to ask this question when she spluttered with rage.

"You said it to scare me, didn't you?"

Hearing what she said with her hands pressing her wound on the stomach, I began to feel disappointed in her.

I hoped it would be all over as soon as possible.

"You murdered one person, but you told us two were dead; the old man was cut thinly, but you said you were cold-blooded. You're not cruel but you ..."

Her second sentence came to me as a flash of lightning, lighting up me inside out. I could no longer hear what she was saying. With half of her mouth in the light of my torch, I could see her lips moving in a way a fish did, as if I was watching a silent movie. It seemed a huge planet was turning slowly in the shadow on her side, to show its mottled surface. I managed to avoid it, but it was so powerful that I turned to it slowly.

It was the reclining chair. And the old man on it.

All memories coming flooding back that I had tried to blot out disappeared all at once. The chair was in the shadow where the darkness met the lightness. I didn't need to use my torch, but it was becoming clearer and clearer in my eyes.

On the chair was the desiccated corpse of the man, whose mouth was half-open to show his dirty teeth. I knew it had been how he died. He had remained on the chair even after the earthquake that had rocked the place. I had never expected it was the way he died! He had not been tied, nor had he lost any of his organs. The only wound, which Zhong Yi had told me about, was a scar across his chest, but it seemed only a scratch and was almost invisible.

It was only a superficial cut, rather than the numerous stabs as I had remembered.

I stared at the wound, and it seemed I could see the inside of it. I could see blood oozing from the wound. I was led by the blood through the many twisted memories of mine of the past.

What had happened that afternoon was back to me.

I was walking between shelves in the treasure room, toward someone who was moaning and groaning at the end.

Finally, I saw him, a naked old man who sat in an armchair, his clothes beside him. He rubbed his face with a white jade statue held in one hand and played with himself with the other hand. His face flushed scarlet with excitement, his eyes tightly closed and his mouth wide-open.

I was shocked to see what was happening before my eyes. The first time I had met him, he had been studying the statue of the girl, saying it was a jade spirit, with which he would be able to find quality jade. Later he told me I should pay my respects to her, which I did from the bottom of my heart. I started to treat her as part of my life, which the old man could never do. From time to time, I would take her home with genuine sincerity, carrying her on a piece of clean cloth spread on my hands and speaking to her.

Later, I had finally realized that what he had referred to as a "spirit" had been nothing to him. But I loved her, and I believed she was full of life. She watched me from behind her half-closed eyelids.

I had never expected that the dirty old man would do what he was doing. What the hell was he doing?

I began to tremble uncontrollably in astonishment, which caused the shelf beside me to move and a precious raw white jade material fell down with a bump. The man jerked before lying motionless, his heavy breathing becoming sharp and piercing gasping for air, which soon was replaced by a gargling noise from his throat.

I was frozen in horror, as he struggled desperately to raise his head before he moaned and groaned. Frightened out of my wits, I turned to run away. Several shelves were knocked flying and I stumbled and fell. As I was trying to rise to my feet, the moaning stopped and then my name was called in a coarse, angry voice.

Turning my head, I saw he finally tilted his head up, but his face was deadly pale. He asked me to go over, and I walked up slowly. It took me ages to move the few steps between us. I was approaching him when he pulled a knife out of nowhere towards me.

He knew he was dying, but he would rather be buried with all his treasures, instead of allowing them to fall into the wrong hands.

He was approaching death. He thrust the knife with all his strength, but he did it so slowly that I could neatly fend his arm off after I stood aghast for a moment. He was so powerless that I pushed him and his knife turned around to cut himself across his chest before it clattered to the floor.

I saw blood spurting from his chest. It was the first time I saw such frightening blood because it smelled of death. He collapsed into the chair, dead still. I put my hand before his nose and I knew he was dead.

The blood was still spreading, until everything before my eyes was red. I turned and ran out of the room, the house, the city of Kashgar.

As I turned my head to the armchair, I saw "her"—and the white. She fell off the old man's hand and had been lying there for twelve years.

It had been "her," instead of her.

Now I understood that the old man died of orgasm. But I had thought it had been me who killed him, which had filled me with sheer terror. For a long time, when I thought about what had happened, I saw nothing but blood before my eyes, which spattered everything around me.

I had lived in absolute terror and I must find an excuse for doing it, a perfect excuse which would allow me to face myself and to start a new life.

I had brought back bits and pieces of my life in the five years. Hatred had been extracted and a beast was born, which started to talk to me. I came to realize that the old man had been doomed to die and to be killed. Every time I recalled the pools of blood, I found myself enjoying the pleasure of revenge. I began to believe that repeated stabbing was needed for that blood—and for his dreadful crime. I started to write stories about crimes and death. While I felt more relieved as a crime story of mine came out, my memory of the past began to be twisted until I met the old man again. He had only one knife wound on him.

So I didn't kill twelve years ago.

I didn't kill. A voice inside me repeated that I didn't kill. It was like a curse put on me, and I was outside my own control until I saw a flash of cold light before me.

It was Zhong Yi picking up her knife. The light caught the blade with blood, which looked like a broken mirror.

She moved rather slow, slower than the old man who died an insane death during sex.

I watched the knife approaching me, touching my clothes, cutting my skin, and thrusting into my left side between the fourth and fifth ribs.

I didn't feel the pain, but I thought it was all ridiculous.

I laughed. I imagined I was flashing a smile at her.

"It would be a fascinating story," I said.

But I had no idea whether she could hear me.

Stories by Contemporary Writers from Shanghai

A Nest of Nine Boxes
Jin Yucheng

A Pair of Jade Frogs
Ye Xin

Ah, Blue Bird
Lu Xing'er

All the Way to Death
Na Duo

Aroma's Little Garden
Qin Wenjun

Beautiful Days
Teng Xiaolan

Between Confidantes
Chen Danyan

Breathing
Sun Ganlu

Calling Back the Spirit of the Dead
Peng Ruigao

Dissipation
Tang Ying

Folk Song
Li Xiao

Forty Roses
Sun Yong

Game Point
Xiao Bai

Gone with the River Mist
Yao Emei

Goodby, Xu Hu!
Zhao Changtian

His One and Only
Wang Xiaoyu

Labyrinth of the Past
Zhang Yiwei

Memory and Oblivion
Wang Zhousheng

No Sail on the Western Sea
Ma Yuan

Normal People
Shen Shanzeng

Paradise on Earth
Zhu Lin

Platinum Passport
Zhu Xiaolin

River under the Eaves
Yin Huifen

She She
Zou Zou

The Confession of a Bear
Sun Wei

The Eaglewood Pavilion
Ruan Haibiao

The Elephant
Chen Cun

The Little Restaurant
Wang Anyi

The Messenger's Letter
Sun Ganlu

The Most Beautiful Face in the World
Xue Shu

The 17-Year-Old Hussars
Lu Nei

There Is No If
Su De

Vicissitudes of Life
Wang Xiaoying

When a Baby Is Born
Cheng Naishan

White Michelia
Pan Xiangli